As you probably guessed from the picture, Atticus closely resembles me! I mean me, Henry the cat, not me, Jennifer Gray, the author. I'm thrilled to have so many fans and wanted to let you know that my, I mean, Atticus's new adventure is even funnier and more exciting than the last one. Thanks Jennifer for turning me into an action-cat hero! And thanks, you guys, for reading.

Henry (and Jennifer)

Atticus Claw Breaks the Law

Shortlisted for the
Waterstones Children's Book Prize

'Atticus is the coolest cat in the world.
This is the coolest book in the world.'
Lexi, age 7

'Atticus Claw is fantastic because it has interesting
creatures and characters. I especially like Atticus.'
Charlotte, age 8

'I think that this book is the best book I've
ever read because it's so funny!'
Yasmin, age 10

'Fun and exciting, Atticus Grammiticus
Cattypuss Claw is the most cutest. Once i
opened it i just couldn't put it down.'
Saamia, age 9

'It's mysterious — it makes you want to
read on.'
Evie, age 7

'Once you start to read it you can't stop!'
Molly, age 8

ATTICUS CLAW

Lends a Paw

Jennifer Gray is a barrister, so she knows how to spot a cat burglar when she sees one, especially when he's a large tabby with a chewed ear and a handkerchief round his neck that says Atticus Claw. Jennifer's other books include *Guinea Pigs Online*, a comedy series co-written with Amanda Swift and published by Quercus. Jennifer lives in London and Scotland with her husband and four children, and, of course, Henry, a friendly but enigmatic cat.

By the same author

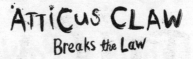

ATTICUS CLAW
Breaks the Law

ATTICUS CLAW
Settles a Score

JENNIFER GRAY

ATTICUS CLAW

Lends a Paw

faber and faber

First published in 2013
by Faber and Faber Limited
Bloomsbury House, 74–77 Great Russell Street,
London WC1B 3DA

Printed in England by CPI Group (UK) Ltd, Croydon, CR0 4YY

A CIP record for this book
is available from the British Library

ISBN 978–0–571–28447–4

FSC
www.fsc.org
MIX
Paper from
responsible sources
FSC® C101712

2 4 6 8 10 9 7 5 3 1

To Andrew and Elizabeth
With special thanks to Flora and Henry

FEATURING!

The goodies

ATTICUS CLAW
The world's greatest REFORMED cat burglar

THE CHEDDAR FAMILY
Inspector Cheddar, Mrs Cheddar, Michael and Callie

MRS TUCKER
The Cheddars' housekeeper, ex-MI6, lives in Toffly Hall with . . .

MR TUCKER
Sailor and beard-jumper-owner

PROFESSOR VERRY-CLEVER
Egyptian expert at the British Museum

NELLIE SMELLIE

Owner of the Littleton-on-Sea Home for Abandoned Cats

BEDAWI

A mysterious Bedouin in the Egyptian desert . . .

And . . .

The baddies

ZENIA KLOB

Ex-KGB, very dangerous

GINGER BISCUIT

Klob's evil cat

THE MAGPIES

Jimmy, Slasher and Thug

LORD AND LADY TOFFLY

The nasty ex-owners of Toffly Hall

Part One
Littleton-on-Sea

Atticus Grammaticus Cattypuss Claw – once the world's greatest cat burglar and now its most brilliant police cat – was excited. It wasn't just because his special friend Mimi, the pretty Burmese, was staying with him and the Cheddar family while her owner, Aisha, was away visiting her mother. It was also because Nellie Smellie, the owner of Littleton-on-Sea Home for Abandoned Cats, had invited him to talk to the new kittens about how to stay out of trouble.

It was Atticus's first official police-catting job, following his recent promotion by Her Majesty the Queen to Police Cat Sergeant for stopping a gang of villains from stealing the Crown Jewels. He felt proud to be able to lend a paw.

Inspector Cheddar dropped him off at the gate in the panda car. 'Remember, Atticus,' he said, 'Cats are like criminals: you can't trust them. Especially this lot.'

Atticus frowned. It was annoying that Inspector Cheddar still didn't like cats, even after all Atticus had done to help him out! And it wasn't the kittens' fault they were homeless: they had been turfed out when Bigsworth Cats' Home had closed down and they had nowhere else to go.

'But these kittens look up to you,' Inspector Cheddar continued. 'You can make a difference. Answer all their questions. And think of something fun for them to do to keep them off the streets.' He practised a few karate chops. 'I always tell kids exercise is the best thing. You should try that with the kittens.'

'Meow!' Atticus hopped out of the panda car. His police cat badge was pinned to the red handkerchief he wore round his neck. He rubbed it  shiny with his cheek, quickly groomed his black-and-brown-striped fur and checked his white paws were clean. He'd show Inspector Cheddar he was wrong about cats. The kittens wouldn't be any trouble once Atticus had given his talk. He walked up the path importantly, holding his tail high.

Nellie Smellie was waiting for him at the front door with her knitting. 'This way, Police Cat Sergeant Claw.' She led the way through the house, knitting needles clicking furiously. (The Littleton-on-Sea Home for Abandoned Cats was really just *her* home, full of stray cats.) Atticus followed a safe distance behind. Nellie Smellie was very old and smelt of mothballs and cat wee. She had a face like a tortoise and always wore the same long black skirt, mildewed white blouse and green cardigan with holes in the elbows. She was also so busy concentrating on her knitting that she was likely to tread on your tail if you weren't careful.

The good thing about Nellie Smellie though was that, unlike Inspector Cheddar, she absolutely adored cats.

'Here we are!' Nellie Smellie opened the door to the sitting room. The room was full of kittens. They lounged about, ripping the stuffing out of the sofas and watching TV. One of them was sharpening its claws with a penknife. He reminded

Atticus of his arch-rival, Ginger Biscuit, when *he* was a kitten.

Atticus touched his chewed ear: Biscuit had bitten it when they became enemies. But Atticus had got his revenge. Thanks to him, Biscuit and his evil owner, Zenia Klob, mistress of disguise, were holed up thousands of miles away in Siberia with Jimmy Magpie and his gang of thieving birds. *That would teach Biscuit and his pals to try and steal the Crown Jewels when Atticus Claw was on the case!* Atticus thought. He relaxed. Compared to Biscuit and the magpies, a bunch of kittens would be a piece of steak.

'I'll leave you to it.' Nellie Smellie switched off the TV. 'If you need me I'll be in the kitchen showing my abandoned lady cats' group how to knit.' She shuffled out, her long black skirt rustling.

There was silence.

'Soooooooo,' Atticus said. 'Here we all are.'

The kittens stared at him frostily.

'I'm here to talk to you about being good,' he began.

The kittens yawned. Some of them sat back and folded their paws across their chests.

'It's good to be good.' Atticus swallowed nervously.

'Why is it?' asked the mean-looking kitten.

'Because it's better than being bad.' Atticus cleared his throat. This wasn't going very well.

'Is it true you used to be a cat burglar?' one of the kittens asked.

'Er . . .' Atticus didn't know what to say. Then he remembered Inspector Cheddar had told him to answer all their questions. 'Yes,' he admitted. 'The world's greatest.'

The kittens looked more interested.

'When did you learn?' a second kitten asked.

'When I was about the same age as you,' Atticus told her.

'Who taught you?'

'A cat called Ginger Biscuit. We both worked for a criminal called Klob.'

'How many things did you steal?' a third kitten demanded.

'Um . . . hundreds, probably. Thousands even. I didn't keep count.'

7

'What sort of things?'

'Well, you know . . . diamonds rubies, pearls, watches – that kind of thing.'

'How come you never got caught?'

'Because I always gave the police the slip,' Atticus said. It was true. He always did. 'And I never left any clues.'

What was the most valuable thing you stole?

Where did you live?

How did you get in and out?

Did you ever meet anyone famous?

The questions came thick and fast. Atticus answered them. The kittens seemed really interested in what he had to say.

'Why have you got a chewed ear?' the mean-looking one asked.

'I got into a fight with Ginger Biscuit.'

'Cool!' several of them shouted.

'Not really,' Atticus said. He hated violence.

'Can you teach *us* to be cat burglars?' the mean-looking one said slyly.

'Kitty please?' another begged.

'Teach us! Teach us!' The kittens chanted.

'NO!' Atticus shouted. This was going all wrong.

The kittens looked sulky.

'Look,' Atticus said, 'it's not a *good* thing to be a cat burglar. That's what I've been trying to tell you. It's not something to be proud of! That's why I stopped. It makes people sad when you steal things. And you could end up in prison. What's the point in that?'

The kittens were quiet.

'But there's nothing to do around here,' the mean-looking one complained. 'It's *boring*!'

Atticus remembered the other thing Inspector Cheddar had told him. 'Do some exercise,' he said.

The kittens looked disgusted.

'It's fun!' said Atticus. (*Was it?* he wondered. *He'd never done any.*)

'We hate exercise,' the kitten said.

'Well, do something else, then,' Atticus replied, exasperated.

'Like what?' the kitten started chewing a bit of sofa stuffing.

Suddenly Atticus remembered a TV ad he'd seen for cat food. It had featured a happy-looking kitten climbing trees, exploring and playing with balls of wool while its owner looked on lovingly.

'Climb trees!' he said confidently. 'Go exploring! Play with balls of wool! Trust me, you'll love it.'

The kittens looked at one another and shrugged.

'Okay,' they agreed moodily. 'If you say so.' They got down off the sofas and slouched into the hall. Then they disappeared, one by one, through the cat flap.

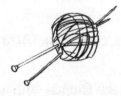

After the talk, Atticus met Mimi at the beach and they went for a stroll along the sand.

'How was it?' Mimi asked.

'Great!' Atticus said. 'I really think I got through to them. I don't think they'll cause any trouble. They'll be too busy doing all the fun things I suggested.'

'Good,' Mimi said. 'Inspector Cheddar will be pleased.'

They stopped to make friends with a small child who gave them some ice cream and sat in the sun by the beach hut for a while.

They got back to number 2 Blossom Crescent at teatime. Atticus was pleased to find the kids were working on their holiday project. It was about him.

Well, not about him *exactly*. But about cats who lived in an age when they were actually *appreciated* by humans, instead of being told to get off the sofa and stop scratching the rug, which is what Inspector Cheddar kept telling Atticus to do.

'Mum, did you know that the Ancient Egyptians worshipped cats?' Callie was doing some research on the computer.

Atticus purred. He imagined lying on a large velvet sofa waving a regal paw while Inspector Cheddar brought him sardines on a gold cat dish. He let out a heavy sigh. The chances of that actually happening in real life were zilch.

'They had a cat goddess called Bastet.'

Bastet? It sounded like 'basket' without the *k*. Talking of baskets, Aisha had forgotten to bring Mimi's when she dropped her off, so Mimi had curled up in *his* basket by the fridge. (Atticus was sleeping in Inspector Cheddar's favourite armchair while she stayed, although obviously he hadn't let Inspector Cheddar find out!)

'They kept cats as pets too,' Michael said. He was drawing a picture of an Egyptian cat. 'They were tabbies, like Atticus.' He showed Atticus his drawing.

Atticus purred throatily. The cat was very like him, all the way down to its white socks. The only difference was it didn't have a chewed ear or a red handkerchief around its neck with its name on.

'I had an idea about your project.' Mrs Cheddar opened the oven and took out a steaming dish of fish pie. She picked out two of the largest prawns and put them on a saucer to cool, then set them on the floor beside Atticus's basket.

Atticus sniffed. *Prawns!* He liked prawns almost as much as sardines. If Inspector Cheddar ever started to worship him, he must remember to wave for prawns as well. He strolled over to the saucer.

'I was talking to Mr and Mrs Tucker about how to raise money for the Littleton-on-Sea Home for Abandoned Cats,' Mrs Cheddar explained. 'And it turns out that one of the previous owners of Toffly Hall – Howard Toffly – was a famous Egyptologist.'

Mr and Mrs Tucker were friends of Atticus. Mr Tucker was a fisherman. Mrs Tucker had once been a government secret agent called Agent Whelk. They used to live in a cottage by the sea until amazing things had happened (also thanks to Atticus).

They discovered they were very rich and the horrible Lord and Lady Toffly who used to live at Toffly Hall were very poor. So now the Tuckers lived in the Hall and organised events for charity while the Tofflys lived on the caravan site and polished spoons for a living.

'What's an Egyptologist?' Callie asked.

'Someone who explored the pyramids and discovered Ancient Egyptian treasure,' Mrs Cheddar explained.

Atticus was listening so intently he'd forgotten to eat his prawn. Being an Egyptologist sounded even more exciting than being a police cat. He thought he might give it a try.

'That's awesome, Mum!' Michael exclaimed. 'Was he cursed by the pharaohs for disturbing their tombs?'

Atticus's chewed ear drooped. He didn't like the sound of being cursed by a pharaoh. Maybe he'd stick to police-catting after all.

'I don't know,' Mrs Cheddar shivered. 'But we've booked a professor from the British Museum to give a lecture at the Hall about Howard Toffly's adventures. We'll have a collection afterwards and give the money to Nellie Smellie to buy the new kittens something to play with. I thought you two could ask the Professor some questions afterwards about Egyptian cats.'

'Good thinking, Mum,' Michael said.

'That should raise loads of money for the Home for Abandoned Cats.' Callie went to wash her hands.

'WHAT? So those rotten kittens can cause *more* trouble?' a cross voice said.

Atticus looked up. The cross voice belonged to Inspector Cheddar. The Inspector stomped into the kitchen, threw himself down on a chair and took off his cap.

'What's happened?' Mrs Cheddar gasped.

Inspector Cheddar's face was caked in soot from the eyebrows down. His uniform was ripped in several places and there were twigs sticking out of his ears.

'I got hijacked by a bunch of hooli-cats,' Inspector Cheddar stormed.

'What did they do?' Michael asked.

'What *didn't* they do, more like?!' Inspector Cheddar snarled. 'I spent the entire afternoon with the fire brigade trying to get two of them down from a tree. Then we discovered that some of the others had got into my panda car and ripped up all the seats. *Then*, when we'd packed them all back off to the Littleton-on-Sea Home for Abandoned Cats the panda car wouldn't start.'

'Why not?' Mrs Cheddar said.

Inspector Cheddar pulled a ball of wool out of his pocket. 'Because they'd stuck *this* up the exhaust pipe! When I bent down to take a look the blasted thing backfired – BOOM! – right in my face.' Suddenly he rounded on Atticus. 'What did you talk to them about this morning?'

Atticus felt peeved. *Why was Inspector Cheddar blaming him?* He'd told the kittens not to get into trouble, hadn't he? Just like Inspector Cheddar said. He'd answered all their questions and suggested they get some exercise. He'd even given them some fun things to do. He'd told them to climb trees and go exploring. And play with balls of wool . . . *Oops!* Atticus's chewed ear drooped.

'I knew it!' Inspector Cheddar was watching him closely. 'It was your idea!' He bent down, picked up the saucer and swept the prawns into the bin.

'Dad!' the children protested.

Mimi gave a little meow from the basket. One of the prawns was for her!

Inspector Cheddar ignored them. 'No more prawns,' he shouted. 'No more sardines, or cat treats or bits of crispy bacon. Atticus is on dried food from now on until I say otherwise. Perhaps it'll teach *him* to stay out of trouble!'

Atticus's good ear drooped. He hated dried food. It was like mummified rabbit poo. He let out an even heavier sigh. *If only he really was an Ancient Egyptian cat god, like Bastet!*

Atticus squeezed into the ballroom at Toffly Hall with Michael, Callie, Mimi and Inspector and Mrs Cheddar. It was the night of the lecture and the ballroom was packed. Atticus was looking forward to hearing about Howard Toffly. He liked adventure stories (although usually they weren't as exciting as his own adventures).

They made their way through a forest of people to the front row. The kittens were there, with Nellie Smellie and her abandoned lady cats' group who were busy knitting scarves. The kittens gave Atticus a wave. Atticus ignored them. He'd decided not to speak to them again until they'd said sorry for getting him told off. He hopped on to a chair next to Mrs Tucker, trying to look Police-Cat-Sergeant-like.

'Atticus!' Mrs Tucker cried. 'I haven't seen you for ages!' She tickled him under the chin. 'Been keeping out of trouble, I hope?'

Inspector Cheddar was just behind them. He glowered at Nellie Smellie and her cats and ground his teeth at Atticus. He still hadn't got all the soot out of his eyebrows. His police uniform was at the menders.

Atticus's ears drooped.

'I thought not!' Mrs Tucker said cheerfully. 'Trouble seems to follow you around!'

Atticus noticed Mrs Tucker's basket under her chair. There was a delicious smell of sardines coming from it. He looked at it meaningfully.

'Still as greedy as ever, I see!' Mrs Tucker reached into the basket and got out two fish. She gave Atticus and Mimi one each.

Mimi picked at hers delicately. Atticus gulped his down in one before Inspector Cheddar had a chance to stop him. *Greedy!* He was half starved. He hadn't had anything decent to eat for days. He licked his lips and meowed for seconds. When Mrs Tucker ignored him, Mimi gave him the rest of hers.

'Pay attention, Atticus,' Inspector Cheddar

barked. 'It's about to start.'

Atticus settled down for the lecture.

The Professor from the British Museum was sitting at the front of the hall on a podium with Mr Tucker. Behind them was a large screen.

'Huh, hum.' Mr Tucker got to his foot. (He only had one leg because a giant lobster had clipped off the other one once when he was out fishing. Now he had a wooden leg instead.)

The audience went quiet.

'Thank youze for comin' to me house,' Mr Tucker said. 'This is Professor Edmund Verry-Clever and he's here to tell you about shaaarrrks.'

'No he's not, Herman.' Mrs Tucker threw a sardine at her husband. 'He's here to tell us about Howard Toffly, the Egyptologist. What's the matter with you? Have you been on the pickled tuna again?'

Mr Tucker looked confused. He sat down and rubbed his chin.

Atticus watched him, concerned. He knew what was wrong. Normally Mr Tucker had a long beard, which was all tangled up with his smelly jumper (or the other way round). He was very proud of his beard-jumper. He shampooed it regularly with Thumpers' Traditional White Beard Dye and let Atticus groom it for morsels of fish when no one else was looking. But something awful had happened. Ginger Biscuit and the magpies had got stuck in it  when they were trying to escape with the Crown Jewels and Mr Tucker had had to cut it off. *Poor Mr Tucker,* Atticus thought. He definitely wasn't himself without his beard-jumper.

Professor Edmund Verry-Clever stood up. He had long bony fingers, long skinny arms and legs, a long scrawny neck and a big dome-shaped head. Atticus thought he looked very brainy.

'Ladies and gentlemen, children and cats,' the Professor said, 'I am here to tell you about the life of a very special man.' He clicked a button on a remote. The screen behind him changed. A black-and-white photo appeared of a handsome man with a big chin riding an elephant. He had a gun slung over one shoulder and a dead zebra over the other.

'Howard Toffly was an adventurer,' Edmund

Verry-Clever continued. 'He was a man who wrestled lions for entertainment. A man who thought nothing of swimming in a lake full of crocodiles. A man who kept tarantulas instead of loose change in his trouser pockets. A man who travelled around the world on horseback while most people went to Bognor by bus.'

The audience listened, entranced.

Atticus held Mimi's paw.

'Howard Toffly knew no fear,' the Professor said. 'He embraced danger. He laughed in the face of calamity. Until . . .' he paused . . . 'the fateful day he went to Egypt. It was on that day, although he did not know it then, that Howard Toffly was doomed to die a terrible death. Here, in this very house. Cursed for all eternity.'

'Oooohhhh!' said the audience.

'Gaw-blimey!' Mrs Tucker gasped. 'He'd better not have died in my bedroom!'

'His time in Egypt started well enough.' Edmund Verry-Clever threw his hands wide. 'When Howard Toffly took up pyramid raiding, he discovered more tombs and treasure than any Egyptologist before or since. He was the richest, most eligible

22

bachelor in the country. Until . . .' he paused again
. . . 'he heard about the lost city of Nebu-Mau: the
golden city of cats.'

The golden city of cats! This was the best story
Atticus had ever heard! He squeezed Mimi's paw.
Mimi squeezed his back.

Edmund Verry-Clever shook his head sorrowfully. 'Its existence was only a rumour, but Howard
Toffly could not rest until he found it. He spent
years searching the desert. He mapped every journey he took. He researched all the ancient ruins.
Many of his papers can still be found here in the
library at the Hall. But he found nothing. Nothing!
Until . . .' his eyebrows shot up . . . 'he came across
a book.'

A book? Atticus glanced at Mimi. That didn't
sound very exciting.

'This wasn't just any book.' Edmund Verry-
Clever cracked his knuckles. 'This was a book full
of the mysteries of the ancient world. A book
which, for those who could decipher it, told the
way to Nebu-Mau and to the treasures it held.'

'Ooooohhhhh!' sighed the audience.

'Oh my giddy aunt!' Mrs Tucker breathed.

Even the kittens were on the edge of their seats.

'But the book carried with it a terrible prophecy,' Edmund Verry-Clever said solemnly. 'He who disturbed the tomb of the cat pharaoh of the golden city would be cursed by the pharaoh himself.' The Professor took a deep breath. 'One can only assume that Howard Toffly *did* stumble upon the tomb of the cat pharaoh. For *this* is what became of him.'

A new picture flashed up on the screen of an old man in a dressing gown and a pair of fluffy slippers sitting in a wheelchair. He had a paper bag over his head.

'Aaaaahhhh!' the audience gasped.

'You may well say "Aaaaahhhh!",' Edmund Verry-Clever agreed. 'Howard Toffly returned to Toffly Hall a broken man. A fearful man. A man who hated being alone. A man who was terrified of one thing in particular.' Edmund Verry-Clever pointed a long bony finger at the front row. '*CATS!*' he hissed. 'If Howard Toffly knew we were here today raising money for the Littleton-on-Sea Home for Abandoned Cats, he'd have kittens! But that's not the end of the story.'

Atticus's spine was tingling. He was dying to find out what was.

The audience was spellbound.

'One day, ladies and gentlemen,' Edmund Verry-Clever continued sombrely, 'Howard Toffly was alone in his bedroom. The chambermaid had gone to fetch him some camomile tea to help him sleep. Suddenly she heard screams!'

Atticus's fur stood on end. Mimi clutched his paw.

Michael and Callie were white.

Mrs Cheddar looked terrified.

Mrs Tucker was hiding behind a sardine.

Even Inspector Cheddar was hooked.

'She ran back to the bedroom as fast as she could. But it was too late. Howard Toffly was dead. The paper bag had been ripped from his head and there were claw marks around his neck.' Edmund Verry-Clever's voice dropped to a tiny whisper. 'The curse had come to claim him.'

'Hhhhuuuuuhhh!' The audience gasped.

'The book was never found.' The Professor put his hands together and bowed his head. 'Some say it was destroyed; others that it remains hidden here, at Toffly Hall. But woe betide he or she who finds it. For they too will be cursed if they use it to find the lost city of Nebu-Mau and disturb the tomb of the cat pharaoh.'

He sat down.

There was complete silence for a few seconds then a burst of applause and cheering.

'Jolly good,' Inspector Cheddar shouted. 'Even though it is complete rubbish,' he added under his breath.

'Don't say that!' Mrs Tucker reached behind and prodded him hard in the ribs with a sardine. She was very superstitious. 'What if the cat pharaoh's listening?! You might be cursed like Howard Toffly.'

'There's no such thing as the curse of the cat pharaoh!' Inspector Cheddar chuckled. 'Honestly, some people are so gullible!'

Professor Verry-Clever waited for the applause to die down. 'Thank you very much, ladies and gentlemen.' He glanced at his watch. 'We still have a bit of time left. Does anyone have any questions?'

To Atticus's surprise, Nellie Smellie had stopped knitting. Her hand shot up.

'Yes, you there: the old lady in the front who looks like a tortoise,' the Professor said pleasantly.

'Howard Toffly wasn't dead when the chambermaid found him,' Nellie Smellie said. 'He was still alive . . . just.'

'How do *you* know?' Edmund Verry-Clever frowned.

'Because I was there!' Nellie Smellie grinned toothlessly. 'I was the chambermaid who found him.'

The Professor's jaw dropped.

So did the rest of the audience's, including Atticus's. A bit of sardine fell off his whisker on to the floor.

'*And* I know where the book is.' Nellie Smellie's tortoise head nodded up and down.

Edmund Verry-Clever practically swooned. 'Where?' he cried. 'Where?'

'Before he died, the master told me he'd hidden the book in the crypt he'd built for himself on the island in the lake. Right here in the grounds of the Hall. The book is in a secret place in a secret chamber where no one can find it.'

Suddenly there was a commotion at the back of the room.

Atticus looked round.

It was Lord and Lady Toffly! They had sneaked into the ballroom late to listen to the lecture.

'That book belongs to us!' Lady Toffly shrieked, waving a spoon in the air.

'Quite right, Antonia.' Lord Toffly's eyes bulged. 'It's mine! I mean ours! And I'm going to get it. Right now. Someone lend me a torch.'

'Oh no you're not!' Mrs Tucker was on her feet. 'If that book belongs to anyone, it belongs to the Egyptian government. You two aren't getting your greedy hands on it. Anyway, I say leave well alone. What's buried is buried.'

'Hear, hear!' the audience cried.

'Meow!' Atticus thought so too. The idea of creeping about in a crypt looking for a book full of Ancient Egyptian mysteries made his fur crawl.

'So push off back to the caravan park, you two!' Mrs Tucker bellowed at the Tofflys. 'Before Mr Tucker throws his wooden leg at you. And take your spoons with you.'

'Hurray!' shouted the audience. This was turning out to be a good evening's entertainment.

'You haven't heard the last of this!' Lady Toffly

gnashed her horsey teeth at Mrs Tucker.

'We'll be back!' Lord Toffly fumed. His face was scarlet. 'You can count on it!'

'Boo!' hissed the audience. 'Boo!'

The Tofflys disappeared.

'Well!' Mrs Tucker sank back into her chair and fanned herself with one of the kittens. 'That was unexpected!' She shook her head. 'I've got a bad feeling about this curse of the cat pharaoh business. I can always sense when there's going to be trouble.' She glanced at Atticus. 'Especially when it's to do with cats.'

4

In Siberia, the weather had turned warmer. It was only minus thirty degrees centigrade, up from minus thirty-one the day before.

Gulag Cottage was covered in snow. Icicles dangled from the roof. A vicious wind howled. So did the hungry wolves in the forest that surrounded it.

Inside the cottage Ginger Biscuit lay on a bearskin rug in front of a roaring log fire, picking bits of bear meat out of his teeth with his claws. Zenia Klob was out pike fishing. The six magpies huddled together under a pile of blankets, moaning.

'I c-c-can't t-t-take th-th-this any m-m-more!' Thug shivered. He used to be fat with missing tail feathers.

Now he was thin with missing tail feathers. 'M-m-my f-f-feathers are f-f-freezing.'

'Your f-f-feathers are f-f-freezing?!' Jimmy Magpie repeated. His eyes had lost their glitter and his glossy wings and tail didn't shine blue and green like they used to. 'Wh-wh-what about m-m-my f-f-feet?'

'M-m-my eyeballs are i-i-icy!' Slasher spluttered. He was scrawnier than ever and his hooked foot ached with the cold.

'I've g-g-got f-f-frostbeak!' Gizzard choked.

'I p-p-pong like a p-p-penguin!' Wally wailed, sniffing his wingpits.

As you can see it took the magpies a very long time to have a conversation in Siberia.

'Y-y-you always p-p-pong, Wal!' Pig's teeth chattered.

'Chaka-chaka-chaka-chaka-chaka!' The magpies fell to squabbling. It was the only thing that kept them warm.

'Shut up!' Ginger Biscuit roared. 'I'm trying to digest bear meat here.'

'What are we gonna do, Jimmy?' Slasher whispered. 'This place is like a prison camp. Zenia treats us like slaves.'

'There's nothing we *can* do,' Jimmy snapped.

'There's not much "we" about it,' Pig grumbled. 'You don't do anything!'

'That's because I'm the boss.' Jimmy gave him a peck.

'If Zenia makes me clean her poo-bucket one more time, I'll be sick,' Thug sobbed.

'If I have to eat another bowl of her fish-scale gruel, so will I!' Gizzard wept.

'C H A K A - C H A K A - C H A K A - C H A K A - CHAKA!' Jimmy silenced them with an angry burst of chattering. 'Get used to it. We're stuck here. Until the next job. When we've done that, we'll go home.'

The mention of 'home' was too much for the magpies.

'I wish I was back in Littleton-on-Sea chasing baby robins,' Pig sniffed.

'I want to poo on clean washing!' Wally snivelled.

'I miss our old nest under the pier!' Slasher sobbed.

Suddenly Thug lost it. He jumped

32

out from under the blanket and ran up and down squawking. Then he threw himself on his stomach and beat his wings on the floor. 'I hate it here!' he shrieked. 'I can't take it any more! I want to go home! Whaaaaaaahhh! Whaaaaaaaahhh!'

'Having a tantrum won't help, you birdbrain!' Jimmy Magpie gave Thug a vicious kick in the crop. 'Get a grip.'

'Yeah, shut up or I'll eat you.' Biscuit rolled over and pinned Thug. He sat up on his muscular haunches and started tossing the magpie from one paw to the other.

'Help!' Thug screeched, flying through the air. 'Help!'

'I've been learning to juggle.' Biscuit grinned, grabbing Wally and Pig. 'It gives me something to do when I'm not killing bears. See?' Soon he had the three magpies flipping round in a circle.

'This is all Atticus Claw's fault,' Slasher complained bitterly. 'If it wasn't for him we wouldn't be in this mess.'

'I told you not to say that name in front of me!'

Biscuit stopped juggling. The three magpies fell on the rug in a heap. 'Next time I see that cat,' Biscuit snarled, 'I'm going to rip his whiskers out and use them to floss my teeth.'

'Let's make his tail into a toilet brush for Zenia to use,' Jimmy cawed.

Thug crawled back under the blanket. 'C-c-can I make a nest snuggler out of the rest of him?' he stammered. 'I n-n-need a f-f-furry one.'

Just then the door flew open.

Squeak . . . squeak . . . squeak.

Zenia Klob blew in, covered in snow. She was wearing her Siberian hunting outfit: fur boots, fur coat, fur gloves and fur knickers (although luckily you couldn't actually see those). She even had a fur squeaky wheelie trolley rather than the usual plastic one. It was full of pike from her fishing trip. Their bloodstained heads poked out from the top.

'I wish she'd get that thing oiled!' Gizzard complained. 'I can't stand the noise it makes.'

'I can't stand the noise *you* make,' Wally retorted. 'Chaka-chaka-chaka-chaka-chaka!'

Zenia lashed at the magpies with her fishing rod.

'No squawking unless I say so!' she yelled. She turned to Biscuit and gave him a sickly smile. 'Here ve are, my bear-killing beauty!' She twisted the head off one of the pike and tossed it to him. Biscuit chomped it. MUNCH! BUURRRP! A horrible fishy smell wafted round the room.

'Good boy!' Zenia crooned. 'I'll let you have the tail later. The rest of you beastly birds can have some of my delicious fish-scale gruel.' She strode into the kitchen dragging the trolley.

Gizzard started to cry.

BANG. BANG. BANG.

'What was that?' Biscuit started.

BANG. BANG. BANG.

Someone or something was banging on the front door of Gulag Cottage.

'We never get visitors here!' Thug whimpered. 'What if it's a yeti?'

'Don't say that!' Ginger Biscuit said.

'Oh yeah,' Wal jeered. 'We forgot you were afraid of monsters.'

'And ghosts!' Pig chuckled. 'Whoooooooo! Whoooooooo!'

'Shut up!' Ginger Biscuit yelled.

'PIPE DOWN, BIRDIES!' Zenia Klob was back. 'I'll deal with it.' She had taken off her hat. Her hair was full of sharp pins, which she dipped in sleeping potion every morning and night. Hairpins were one of her favourite weapons from the days when she was a Russian KGB spy. 'Come in!' she called.

The door swung open. Two human-shaped blocks of ice slid into the room and smacked on to the floor.

'Biscuit, fetch the blowtorch!'

Ginger Biscuit reached into a drawer for the blowtorch and sparked it up from the fire.

Klob got to work defrosting the visitors. After a little while, a fat man wearing a tweed suit slithered from the first block of ice while a tall woman with horsey teeth and knobbly knees spilled out of the second.

'I know them!' Thug whispered. 'They're the Tofflys!'

'They killed Beaky!' Slasher squawked.

It was true. Some time ago, Lord and Lady Toffly had run over the magpies' friend Beaky in their Rolls-Royce. Beaky's death was what tipped the magpies from being just plain nasty to a life of crime: Jimmy had decided it was time to get even with human magpie-mashers. That's when he'd enlisted the help of Atticus – then the world's greatest cat burglar. But Atticus had changed his mind and decided to go straight.

'Should we poo on them, Boss?' Wally asked. He waggled his backside and let out a rude noise.

'Wait!' Jimmy hissed. 'Let's see what they want. They might be able to help us get out of this joint. *Then* we'll poo on them.'

The visitors struggled to their feet.

'We're Lord and Lady Toffly,' the woman introduced herself to Zenia Klob. 'Are you Miss Klob?'

'It's Ms, not Miss!' Zenia Klob spat.

'All right! Keep your knickers on!' Lady Toffly said snootily. 'We want you to help us recover a priceless Egyptian book from Toffly Hall. It's worth zillions.'

'Go on.' Zenia Klob's ears waggled with excitement. She stroked Biscuit.

'GGGGRRRRRR!' Biscuit liked the sound of it too. Toffly Hall was where those horrible friends of Claw lived: Mr and Mrs Tucker. He still had nightmares about being tangled up in Mr Tucker's beard-jumper. This could be his chance to get back at the Tuckers and finish Atticus off once and for all.

The magpies listened carefully, their heads on one side.

'I wish I had my shotgun!' Lord Toffly said, eyeing them.

'Not now, Roderick!' Lady Toffly snapped. 'This is business, not pleasure. The book belonged to our ancestor, Howard Toffly, the famous Egyptologist,' she explained. 'It will lead us to the lost city of Nebu-Mau: the golden city of cats, and to the treasure of the cat pharaoh himself.'

'Vow!' Zenia breathed. 'The lost city of Nebu-Mau! That sounds tempting, doesn't it, Biscuit? I've alvays vanted to try out my mummy disguise.'

'The book is in a secret hiding place in a secret chamber in Howard Toffly's crypt,' Lady Toffly said.

'The crypt is on an island in the lake,' Lord Toffly added. 'In the grounds of Toffly Hall.'

'Ginger von't have any problem vith that.' Zenia Klob smiled. 'Vill you, my little crypt cracker? I'll drop him off in the boat. He'll be in and out in a visker.'

POP. POP. POP. POP. Biscuit popped out his claws one by one.

Lady Toffly shook her head. 'Breaking into the crypt is a job for those mangy magpies.' She lowered her voice. 'There's a curse, you see. Anyone who disturbs the cat pharaoh is doomed, like Howard Toffly. He was horribly murdered in his bed.'

Ginger Biscuit withdrew his claws.

Thug fainted.

Wally pooed himself.

'We reckon magpies being what they are . . .' Lady Toffly continued –

'Revolting,' Lord Toffly sneered –

'. . . they're the best ones to steal the book.'

'Vy?' asked Zenia.

'They're a bad omen,' Lady Toffly told her. 'People are superstitious

about them. They've got the whiff of evil. So they're less likely to offend Anubis, the Egyptian God of the Underworld.' Lady Toffly snickered. 'Hopefully Anubis won't even bother to wake up his cat pharaoh pal to tell him the book's gone missing again if the magpies take it. And *if* the magpies are still alive by the time we get to Egypt, they can lead the way into the cat pharaoh's tomb as well. Anubis won't suspect a thing.' She flashed her horsey teeth in a yellow grin.

'And even if old Nuby *does* tell on them to the pussycat king,' Lord Toffly sniggered, 'what Antonia and I say is, let's get the curse out of the way by bringing it down on the magpies first! Then the rest of us can schmooze in and steal all the treasure while the cat pharaoh's busy ripping the magpies' throats out. Then *we* can turf out the Tuckers and return to Toffly Hall and *you* can put some central heating in this dump. What d'you reckon, *Ms* Klob?'

'Great idea!' Zenia shouted. 'Brilliant, in fact. Let's get the burnt beetroot out and celebrate! Vait a minute!' Her eyes narrowed. 'Never mind the curse! Ve'll have to vatch out for Inspector Cheddar and his cheesy family. And those vorms, the Tuckers. And that traitorous veasel, Atticus Claw. Ve don't vant them spoiling the plan like they did last time!'

'GGGGGRRRRR!' Biscuit started wrestling with the bearskin, pretending it was Atticus.

'We've already thought of that,' Lady Toffly said smoothly. 'We're going to create a diversion to put Cheddar off the scent. Show them, Roderick.'

Lord Toffly reached into his coat pocket and pulled out a fist full of knitting needles, some balls of wool and a screwed-up magazine cutting.

Klob, Biscuit and the magpies looked at the Tofflys, bewildered.

'Vot's that for?' Klob demanded.

'Are we going to knit nest snugglers?' Thug woke up.

Lord Toffly winked. 'Let's just say we've got it covered!' He uncurled the magazine cutting and spread it on the table.

THUMPERS' KNITQUICK

from the Makers of Traditional Beard-Dyeing Products Comes a Revolutionary New Knitting Needle Lotion with Added Oil of Ewesmilk. Reach Speeds of a Thousand Stitches per Second! Knit Jumpers in an Instant!

Thumpers' Knitquick: for All Your Speed-Knitting Needs

Lord Toffly embraced his wife. 'We're going to knit the town red!'

Inspector Cheddar was baffled. Littleton-on-Sea was under siege. Four graffiti knitting crimes in as many days! It was the worst crime spree the town had known since Atticus had stopped being a cat burglar and got rid of the magpies.

The first day Inspector Cheddar woke up to find his panda car wearing a knitted cover that said 'GET LOST, LOSER'. The next day he was called to a park where the roundabout had been stitched up. On the third day, startled shopkeepers in Littleton-on-Sea on their way to work reported that the town-hall clock sported a woolly hat. On the fourth day the pier had disappeared beneath a very large pair of red knitted underpants.

'What's going on, Cheddar?'

Inspector Cheddar was in the Chief Inspector of Bigsworth's office. The Chief Inspector was purple in the face from shouting at him.

'I don't know, sir,' Inspector Cheddar admitted.

'You don't know?' the Chief Inspector roared. 'What good's that?'

'None, sir,' Inspector Cheddar said.

'We need to find out who's behind this evil crime,' the Chief Inspector yelled.

'Yes, sir.'

'They're making the police look ridiculous!'

'Yes, sir.'

'We can't have police officers driving round in woolly panda cars saying 'GET LOST, LOSER'. What if the papers got hold of it?'

Inspector Cheddar agreed that would be a disaster.

'Think, Cheddar! Who do you know in Littleton-on-Sea who knits?'

Inspector Cheddar thought for a moment. 'Nellie Smellie, the old lady who runs the cats' home does,' he said doubtfully. 'She organises an abandoned lady cats' knitting circle. But I don't think that she—'

'Shut up!'

'Yes, sir.'

'I don't care what you think!'

'But you just said . . .'

The Chief Inspector silenced him with a look.

'This Smellie Nellie woman: is she a known criminal?'

'No, sir.'

'Hmmm. Just as I suspected: that makes it easier for her to slip under our radar.'

'That's true, sir,' Inspector Cheddar agreed. 'But she must be about a hundred and seven. I don't think she could climb the town-hall clock to put a hat on it.'

'She must have an accomplice then. Maybe more than one. What about those kittens? Didn't you say you'd had some trouble with them?'

Inspector Cheddar stared at the Chief Inspector. What he was saying was beginning to make sense. 'You're right, sir, I did! In fact now you come to mention it, they can climb! I had to get the fire brigade out last week to help me get them down from a tree.'

'Go on!' the Chief Inspector was listening intently.

'After that I found the other kittens in the panda car ripping the seats,' Inspector Cheddar told him. 'And THEN they stuffed a ball of wool up the exhaust pipe! It was Atticus's idea.'

'What? You're saying Police Cat Sergeant Claw's behind it?' the Chief Inspector thundered. 'He should be thrown out of the force.'

'No, I didn't mean that!' Inspector Cheddar said hastily. He trusted Atticus enough to know that he wouldn't go back to a life of cat crime. 'I think he might have given the kittens the idea by mistake.'

'That's the sort of mistake that gets you fired!' The Chief Inspector banged his fist on the desk. 'My gut feeling is Smellie's the one to watch.' He frowned. 'How did she get her hands on so much wool though?'

'The fundraiser!' Inspector Cheddar cried. 'My wife organised a lecture at Toffly Hall to raise money so that Smellie could buy things for the kittens to play with. She raised over two hundred pounds.'

'You mean your wife's in on it?' the Chief Inspector of Bigsworth wriggled his eyebrows. 'That's not good.'

'No, of course she's not!' Inspector
Cheddar said impatiently. 'Smellie must
have used her in her evil knitting plan. Good
heavens,' he cried. 'Is there nothing that woman
wouldn't do?'

The Chief Inspector of Bigsworth shook his
head sorrowfully. 'I'm afraid some criminals are
like that, Cheddar!' he said. 'Lowlife scum.'

'But how do we prove it, sir?' Inspector Cheddar
asked. 'We haven't found so much as a dropped
stitch at the scene, let alone anything incriminating
like a knitting needle we can trace back to the cats'
home.'

'We need to catch those kittens red-pawed,' the
Chief Inspector said. He narrowed his eyes. 'My
guess is they'll strike again, and soon.'

Inspector Cheddar stood up. 'Don't worry, sir.
I'll put my best officers on it straight away. We'll
keep Smellie and her gang under twenty-four-hour
police surveillance. Then, when they strike, we'll
pounce.'

'Make sure you do,' the Chief Inspector said
darkly. 'Or I'll put you back on traffic cones.'

Atticus was put on night watch.

'I can't believe the kittens would do such a thing,' Mimi said to him before he left.

'Neither can I,' Atticus agreed. 'They're not that bad.'

'And Nellie Smellie seems so kind!' Mimi said. 'Do you really think she and her lady cats are master knitting criminals?'

'Not really,' Atticus said.

Mrs Cheddar and Mrs Tucker, who had come round to number 2 Blossom Crescent to say hello, thought the same thing.

'You're being an idiot, darling!' Mrs Cheddar said cheerfully to her husband as she handed Inspector Cheddar his police cap.

'As usual!' Mrs Tucker muttered.

'It's not the kittens, Dad,' Callie and Michael agreed. 'Nellie Smellie's been framed.'

'The question you should be asking yourself is why,' Mrs Cheddar said.

'And by whom,' Mrs Tucker scratched her head.

'Thanks for the advice but *I'll* do the detective work around here,' Inspector Cheddar snapped. He went out of the door.

'Meow!' Atticus winked at Mimi. He had plans to do a bit of detective work of his own.

Atticus and Inspector Cheddar drove to the Littleton-on-Sea Home for Abandoned Cats in Mrs Cheddar's car so that Nellie Smellie wouldn't suspect anything. Inspector Cheddar parked on the opposite side of the road and got out his night-vision binoculars.

'Now listen, Atticus,' Inspector Cheddar said. 'I've got officers on the roof.' He waved at two men dressed in black who were hanging on to the chimney. 'And I've got officers all the way down the street.' A few car windows opened and fists appeared giving the thumbs-up sign. 'I've got officers guarding every public building from Littleton-on-Sea to Bigsworth. No one can get past us. Your job is to guard the back garden in case they go out that way. You got that?'

'Meow,' Atticus said.

'Good. And don't let on that we're here.'

'Meow.'

'Okay, off you go.'

Atticus jumped out of the car and slunk across the road. Nellie Smellie's house had a gate at the side that led to the back garden. Atticus squeezed under it and followed the path round to the back of the house. A light was shining from the sitting room. Atticus jumped up on the window ledge. The kittens were in there, but to his surprise they weren't lounging about watching TV. They were crowded round the table doing a jigsaw. Atticus tapped on the window with his claws.

The mean-looking kitten opened it.

'Hi!' He looked pleased to see Atticus. 'Police Cat Sergeant Claw! Where's your badge?'

Inspector Cheddar had made Atticus take it off for the surveillance operation, although he still had his neckerchief on.

'I'm incognito,' Atticus said.

'In where?' The kitten looked blank.

'You're not supposed to know I'm here,' Atticus explained.

'Oh. Why are you telling me then?'

'Because I want a straight answer,' Atticus said gruffly. He jumped down off the window ledge into the room.

The kittens stopped doing the jigsaw and looked at him.

'Is Nellie Smellie behind the graffiti knitting crime wave?' Atticus demanded.

'Of course not!' the kittens said.

'So you lot aren't accomplices then?'

'No!' the kittens denied.

'Why should I believe you,' Atticus said crossly, 'after what you did the other day?'

The kittens hung their heads.

'We thought you told us to!' the mean-looking one protested.

Atticus growled.

'All right, we didn't really,' the kitten admitted. 'We're sorry we got you into trouble. We won't do it again.'

'Apology accepted,' Atticus said. 'What's with the jigsaw?'

'Nellie bought us some fun things to do with the money from the lecture!' Another kitten pointed to a pile of board games and some packs of cards in the corner. 'Would you like to play something?'

'Another time.' Atticus quickly fitted a piece of jigsaw. 'I've got some police-catting to do.'

'Do you have any leads?' one of them asked.

'Not exactly,' Atticus admitted. 'More of a hunch.' The graffiti knitting had 'magpie' written all over it. It was just the sort of thing they'd do to create a diversion from something else. But Jimmy and his gang were in Siberia with Klob and Biscuit. *Weren't they?*

'Why would someone cover the pier in a giant pair of woolly pants?' The mean-looking kitten frowned. 'And try to blame it on us and Nellie?'

'I don't know.' Atticus scratched his whiskers. He touched his chewed ear. 'But that's exactly what I intend to find out.'

As it happened, Atticus didn't have to wait long.

The next morning Mr Tucker appeared on the doorstep of number 2 Blossom Crescent.

'What are you doing here, Herman?' Mrs Tucker asked. She was looking after the kids for the day while Mrs Cheddar was at work. Inspector Cheddar was at the police station, explaining to the Chief Inspector of Bigsworth why he hadn't caught the graffiti knitter yet. Secretly Inspector Cheddar thought that Atticus might have tipped the kittens off about the surveillance operation. He'd taken him off the case.

'I's thought the kids and Atticus might like a trip on me boat,' Mr Tucker said, looking at the floor. 'See if we can catch us some saaarrrdines.'

'Good idea!' Mrs Tucker said. 'It'll take your mind off your beard-jumper.'

'Can I's take the motorbike?' Mr Tucker asked.

'All right then,' Mrs Tucker agreed. 'Pick me up later.'

Soon Atticus, Mimi, Callie and Michael were tucked into the sidecar. Mr Tucker balanced precariously on the saddle. 'It's haaarrrd to ride a motorbike with a wooden leg,' he grumbled.

They zoomed along Blossom Crescent into Townley Road. They came to a T-junction at the High Street. Mr Tucker turned left.

'Where are we going?' Michael whispered. 'This isn't the way to the sea.'

'This is the way to Toffly Hall!' Callie whispered back.

Atticus was puzzled. *Why would Mr Tucker lie about going for a trip on his boat?* He'd been acting

54

very strangely since his beard-jumper got minced.

They pulled through the gates of Toffly Hall. But instead of going up the main drive towards the house, Mr Tucker turned left along a narrow path through the woods.

They bumped along through the trees. Atticus had never been down here before. The blanket of leaves made everything dark and spooky. After a while they came to a lake. A small rowing boat was tied to a jetty. Mr Tucker stopped the motorbike and switched off the engine.

The children struggled out of the sidecar with Atticus and Mimi.

'Why are we here?' Michael asked.

Mr Tucker pointed across the lake towards an island.

'That's where Howard Toffly's crypt is,' he said.

'But Mrs Tucker said we weren't to go looking for the book!' Callie said, astonished. 'She told us to leave it alone.'

'I's not going after *that* book,' Mr Tucker said. 'I's going after a different book.'

'A different book?' Michael echoed.

'Aye, the one where's I keeps me notes.'

'Your notes?' Callie repeated.

'Aye!' Mr Tucker said impatiently. 'I's been trying to grow me beard-jumper back,' he explained. 'And I's been doing some experiments in secret and keeping all the results in me notebook.' He looked glum. 'I didn't want Edna to find out so I set up a laboratory in the crypt. I knew she wouldn't look for me there! She's funny about dead people, Edna is.'

Atticus knew how Mrs Tucker felt. He was funny about dead people too. Especially when they'd been killed by an Ancient Egyptian curse. He felt his fur prickle.

'Why are you telling *us* then?' Callie asked. 'If it's a secret.'

'Because I keeps forgettin' things!' Mr Tucker rubbed his chin. 'I think one of me blaaarrrsted experiments made me lose me memory. I can't remember where I've put me notebook! And I'm a catfish's whisker away from growing the best beard-jumper ever!'

To Atticus's horror, tears began to drip down Mr Tucker's cheeks. 'I miss me beard-jumper!' he howled. 'I needs youze help!'

'Of course we'll help you, Mr Tucker,' Callie

patted his shoulder. 'I'm sure we'll find your book. You probably put it in a safe place somewhere like Mum does with the car keys.'

'Come on, then!' Michael said. 'What are we waiting for?'

The kids and Mr Tucker stepped into the rowing boat. Mimi followed.

Atticus hung back. It wasn't that he didn't want to help Mr Tucker, but something told him he shouldn't go to the island.

'What is it, Atticus?' Mimi asked. Her golden eyes bored into him.

Atticus shrugged. 'I don't know. Just a feeling.' He shook his head. 'It's nothing.' He hopped into the boat beside Mimi.

The lake was very still. Mr Tucker pulled the boat through the water with the oars. They made a rhythmic splash. A fish jumped. No one spoke. The cats were silent. They were all thinking about Howard Toffly's ancient book and the curse of the cat pharaoh, except Mr Tucker, who was thinking about his beard-jumper.

The island loomed larger as they crossed the lake. It was mostly covered in thick knotty bushes and long grass. A few slender silver birch trees waved like ghostly fingers. No one – other than Mr Tucker – had been near the crypt for years. Atticus swallowed. It wasn't surprising. *Who would want to go there after what happened to Howard Toffly?*

They landed at a small wooden jetty and clambered out of the boat.

'This way!' Mr Tucker limped off.

The children followed with Mimi. Atticus brought up the rear. Thick green moss squelched beneath his paws. Everything about this place was damp and gloomy. Even the stones, which stuck up here and there like grey teeth through the long grass, were covered with lichen.

'Look!' Mimi pointed at one of the stones. It had writing on it.

Atticus's green eyes grew round. It was a gravestone. They were all gravestones! He felt a rising panic. He was surrounded by dead Tofflys! His chewed ear drooped.

'This is it!' Mr Tucker pushed back some tree branches.

The little group stopped dead.

58

Ahead of them was a marble pyramid. In front of the pyramid, as if they were guarding it, sat two large stone statues of cats.

'Howard Toffly's crypt!' Michael breathed.

Atticus stared. There was something familiar about this place. And yet, how could there be? He'd never been here before in his life! He reached out a paw and touched one of the statues gingerly. He felt a flash of energy run through his paw as if he'd had an electric shock. He jumped back, startled. 'Mimi!' he hissed. 'The statue!'

'What about it?' Mimi asked.

'I don't know. I thought I felt something when I touched it.'

Mimi touched the statue carefully. She shook her head. 'It's just stone.'

Atticus felt stupid. This place was really getting to him.

'Come on.' The pyramid had a thick wooden door. It was ajar. Mr Tucker fished in his pocket for a torch and pushed it open. The door creaked. The children stepped in after Mr Tucker. The cats followed. 'Give me a minute,' Mr Tucker said,

flashing the torch beam around. 'While I fires up me generator. I's just need to change the shaaarrrk faaarrrt bottle.'

Shark fart was also the fuel Mr Tucker used to power his fishing boat.

Callie, Michael, Mimi and Atticus stood silently in the gloom while Mr Tucker rattled about with the shark fart canister. Callie reached for Michael's hand. Mimi reached for Atticus's paw.

POOOOOOF!

Suddenly the crypt was filled with light.

They were in a small chamber with an earth floor and marble walls.

The children and the cats stared in astonishment at Mr Tucker's experiments. None of them had expected anything like *this*. Three picnic tables stood in the middle of the chamber, crowded with strange apparatus connected up with tubes. Colourful potions bubbled and fizzed. Clouds of blue gas puffed from a pair of bellows. Weird-looking ingredients spilled from painted jars. Above the picnic tables light bulbs dangled off a looping wire.

'This is me laboratory!' Mr Tucker said.

'Where's Howard Toffly's tomb?' Callie whispered nervously.

'Through there, I suppose.' Mr Tucker pointed to another door in the wall at the back of the chamber. 'But don't worry, youze can't get in.' He chuckled. 'And he can't get out!'

Atticus was relieved to see that the second door was padlocked.

'Where did you get all those jars?' Michael asked.

'I's found them lying about on the flooorrr,' Mr Tucker said. 'They're Ancient Egyptian biscuit tins.'

'No they're not! They're canopic jars,' Michael told him. 'The Ancient Egyptians kept people's brains in them when a corpse was mummified.'

'Oh!' Mr Tucker flicked his false teeth in and out. 'I thought that custard cream I had yesterday was a bit soggy.'

Atticus felt sick.

'Anyways this is what I's working on at the moment!' Mr Tucker said proudly. On one of the picnic tables was a Bunsen burner with a stand around it. Sitting on top of the stand was a glass beaker full of sludge with plastic tubes going in and out in all directions to other bits of equipment.

'Cool!' Michael walked towards it. 'Can you show us how it works?'

'All right.' Mr Tucker lit the Bunsen burner. He handed round four pairs of safety goggles. 'Put these on,' he ordered.

The children and the two cats put them on. Atticus was worried he looked a bit silly but luckily Mimi was too busy watching the experiment to notice.

The contents of the glass beaker started bubbling.

HISS! SPIT! BANG!

The sludge changed from grey to orange to purple.

Drops of liquid dripped in from some of the tubes. Gas ballooned up into others.

'It's me beard-jumper potion,' Mr Tucker explained.

'What's in it?' Callie asked.

'Thumpers' Traditional Beard Grow, mainly,' Mr Tucker said,

'With a pinch of sea salt, saaarrrdine brains, some fabric conditioner, an old sock, cod liver oil, a few flakes of dandruff, a bit of gunpowder and a lock of me old beard-jumper. Then I adds some different beard dyes to get the right colour.'

Mimi looked at Atticus and pulled a face. Atticus tried wriggling an eyebrow back but the plastic safety goggles got in the way.

'Does it work?' Michael asked, fascinated.

'Sort of!' Mr Tucker said. He sat down on a bench and took off his shoe. 'I tried it on me big toe,' he said, peeling off a green-and-blue-striped sock. 'It's as hairy as a pirate's chest. And me sock's involved too, which is good. The only trouble is, me toe's gone stripy!'

'Meow!' Mimi put her paw to her mouth to stop herself laughing. Atticus tried wriggling the other eyebrow.

Mr Tucker's hairy toe was covered in wiry green and blue sock. Either that or Mr Tucker's sock was covered in wiry green and blue toe hair. It was hard to tell them apart.

'That's why I needs me notebook!' Mr Tucker said glumly. 'I need to tweak me measures before I try it with a jumper on me chin.' He pulled his sock and shoe back on.

'Is that all that was left of your old beard-jumper?' Callie asked. The remains of a white fleece were stuffed into a large canopic jar beneath one of the tables.

'Aye!' Mr Tucker said sadly. 'Me beauty!' Suddenly his face changed. He grinned. He guffawed. '*That's* where me notebook is!' he cried. 'I remember now! I wanted to keep it dry so I hid it in there and put me beard-jumper on top of it!' He did a little jig and broke into a sea shanty.

'I'm as happy as a hake with scabies,
I don't care if me dog's got rabies . . .'

'Did you use feathers in the experiment?' Michael interrupted. He bent down beside the jar.

Mr Tucker stopped singing. 'No. Why?'

'Because there are some here.' Michael pointed to a few black-and-white feathers that lay on the ground. Some were edged with blue. Others had a greenish tinge.

'It's those mangy magpies!' Mr Tucker yelled,

pulling the fleece out. The canopic jar was empty. 'They've stolen me notebook!'

'But they're in Siberia!' Callie protested. 'With Zenia Klob and Ginger Biscuit.'

'Not any more, they's not!' Mr Tucker hopped up and down in fury. 'They's back. The Tofflys must have tipped Klob off about the treasure.'

Atticus was listening carefully. *The magpies! So they were back. His hunch had been right! They were the ones trying to frame the kittens. Now he knew why. They wanted to create a diversion and put him and Inspector Cheddar off the scent while they went after Howard Toffly's Ancient Egyptian book! And if the magpies had been here, then Klob and Biscuit couldn't be far away.*

He glanced towards the locked door that led to Howard Toffly's tomb. The ancient book was still in there, somewhere. Once the villains found out they'd stolen the wrong one, they'd be back.

Suddenly Atticus felt a strange sensation, as if he were being pulled towards the locked door. He walked towards it in a trance. *He had to protect the book.*

'Atticus,' Mimi hissed. 'What are you doing?

We have to go. It's time to pick up Mrs Tucker.'

Atticus stopped, confused. He looked back. The kids and Mr Tucker had gone outside. He hadn't even noticed that Mr Tucker had switched off the lights. Mimi was waiting for him. He turned and tried to lift his paws. It was a huge effort: as if he was wading through glue. His paws seemed determined to take him in the other direction: away from Mimi, towards Howard Toffly's tomb and the ancient book.

'Atticus!' Michael stepped back into the pyramid to look for him.

'Atticus!' So did Callie.

Atticus struggled towards them. His legs were like jelly.

'What's wrong with him?' Michael whispered.

Atticus wished he knew himself.

'He looks like he needs help.' Callie moved forward and picked him up. She carried him to the door and put him down gently outside.

Michael stroked him.

Atticus purred weakly.

'Come on, youze lot!' Mr Tucker shouted. 'And don't tell a dover soul about this. If Mrs Tucker finds out what I've been doing, she'll make me cook me own liver for me tea.'

'Coming!' The children hurried off.

The cats followed.

'You sure you're all right?' Mimi whispered.

'Yes.' Atticus was beginning to feel a bit better. He had regained control of his paws.

'I hate this place,' Mimi shivered. 'Don't you?'

Atticus said nothing. He didn't want to worry Mimi, but he knew he had to come back to the island as soon as he got the chance. It was as if some strange inner voice was commanding him to return. *Whatever happened, he had to stop Klob, Biscuit and the magpies getting hold of Howard Toffly's book. Even if it meant stealing it himself.*

Meanwhile, at the caravan park, the magpies were poring over a small hardback book full of strange writing. Zenia, Biscuit and the Tofflys were out at the travel agent's booking cheap flights to Egypt.

'I didn't know they had W. H. Smith in Ancient Egypt,' Slasher said, inspecting the cover.

'They didn't,' Thug said self-importantly. He was the one who'd discovered the notebook under the remains of Mr Tucker's beard-jumper and he was showing off. 'It's code for something else, like "open this and you're dead".'

'Why *aren't* we dead?' Gizzard clutched his throat. 'I thought the Tofflys said the cat pharaoh would munch us when we stole the book.'

'Derr!' Thug jeered. 'Weren't you listening to

what Lord Fatso said?' He looked pained. 'Because we're so evil, we didn't offend the cat pharaoh's pal Anubis, stupid! We're a bad omen – like him. He *loves* us. We're Nube's mates. We're his new *bessies*.'

'All right, Thug, keep your feathers on.' Gizzard pulled an even uglier face than the hideous one he already had. 'I get it.'

'I thought the Ancient Egyptians used hieroglyphs.' Jimmy looked at the W. H. Smith logo suspiciously. 'You know, pictures of things instead of words?'

'Don't worry, it's full of those, Boss,' Thug said eagerly. He opened the book. 'See?'

🧦 + 🐟 + 🪶 + 🍶 = ??

Jimmy flicked through the pages. There were other equations and drawings of peculiar things in bottles including large measures of Thumpers' Traditional Beard Grow.

'Thumpers'...' Jimmy said doubtfully. Zenia had used Thumpers' Traditional Beard Dye on their raven suits for the Crown Jewels job. 'You sure they've been around for four thousand years, Thug?'

'That's why they call it "traditional", Boss.' Thug rolled his eyes at Slasher. He wanted to say 'Derr!' again, but remembered just in time it was Jimmy he was talking to.

'Hmmm . . .' Jimmy blinked. 'How does any of this tell us where to find the lost city of Nebu-Mau?'

'I reckon they're spells,' Thug said. 'You have to do them to find out how to get there.' Thug swished his wings across his face like a magician's cloak then peeled them back, feather by feather. 'Magracadabra!' he cried, gazing upward. 'The path to the golden city is revealed.'

'Maybe there'll be a bright star in the sky?' Gizzard suggested.

'Or a washing line leading the all the way there,' Pig said.

'With clean pants on it!' Thug cackled.

'Or a trail of bird poo,' Wally said. 'Like in *Hansel and Gretel*.'

'Don't be stupid, Wal,' Slasher cawed. 'It was breadcrumbs in *Hansel and Gretel*, not bird poo.'

Jimmy had reached a decision. 'Let's do it.' His eyes gleamed. He examined the drawings in the book closely. 'Pig, put the cooker on.'

Pig flapped on to the kitchen counter and twisted a knob beneath the hob with his beak.

'Shouldn't we wait for Zenia and Biscuit?' Slasher said nervously.

'Chaka-chaka-chaka-chaka-chaka!' Jimmy flew at Slasher. His plumage had regained its normal sheen since they'd left Siberia. He was every inch the gruesome gang leader he had once been.

'Sorry, Boss! I didn't mean it!' Slasher hid behind the other magpies. 'Don't stamp on my hooked foot. Please!'

'Then watch your beak and let me do the thinking round here,' Jimmy hissed. 'Don't you see? If Thug managed to steal Howard Toffly's book without bringing the curse down on us, we can find the golden city on our own. We don't need Klob, Biscuit and the Tofflys. It's us magpies who'll get the treasure. Not *humans*. Or *cats*.' He spat the words out as if they were lemon pips.

'This is our chance to get revenge for Beaky!' Slasher cried. Now he understood.

'And on Klob for making me clean her poo-bucket!' Thug chuckled.

'And on Biscuit for juggling with us!' Pig screeched.

'What about Claw?' Gizzard asked.

'We'll mash him later,' Jimmy said. 'When we've got the treasure. Maybe we can conjure up a curse for him. Like being pecked to death by crows or something. Now let's get on with it.'

'Which spell, Boss?' Thug asked.

'Er . . .' Jimmy hesitated. 'Let's try the one with the sock.'

'We don't have any hair,' Wally complained.

'We can use a bit of Biscuit's,' Slasher suggested. 'He moults all over the place.' He collected some off the carpet in his beak.

'We'll have to use pike instead of sardine,' Gizzard said. 'It's the only fish we've got.'

'Pike's stronger,' Thug said. 'Trust me, it'll be even better.'

'What about the fish oil?' Pig asked.

'Let's squeeze some out of the pike's brains,' Jimmy flexed his claws.

The magpies assembled the ingredients and

placed them on top of the kitchen counter. Luckily Zenia had an old sock that she wore over her head for her bank robber disguise, which Pig found in the washing machine. They put everything into a saucepan and pushed the pan on to the cooker.

Soon the pike head went soggy and mashed into the oil and salt. Together with the hair it made a pleasantly smelly, sticky mixture, but the sock remained stubbornly sock-like.

'We need something to dissolve it,' Jimmy chattered. 'It's no good like that. I'll bet that's what the Thumpers' Traditional Beard Grow is for.'

'What about some feather dye remover?' Wally suggested. 'There's some left over from the Crown Jewels job. It's under the sink.'

'All right,' Jimmy agreed. 'Let's give it a try.'

Soon the mixture looked even better. The sock didn't exactly dissolve, but all the colour came out instead and turned everything sludge brown.

'So . . .' Jimmy eyed the gang. 'Who's going to volunteer?'

All the magpies took a step back.

'I vote Thug should do it,' Gizzard said, 'seeing as how he found the book.'

'Yeah! It's like he's the chosen one,' Slasher agreed. 'No offence, Jimmy,' he added hastily.

'Chaka-chaka-chaka-chaka-chaka!' The other magpies hopped about in agreement.

'What do you say, Thug?' Jimmy put his head on one side and blinked.

'All right.' Thug sighed extravagantly. 'If you think it's my duty.' He gazed skyward at the caravan ceiling. 'Oh great Egyptian bird god, Horus, bring me your magical wisdom!' he prayed. 'Let me be the special magpie who discovers the lost city of Nebu-Mau without getting crushed by the curse of the cat pharaoh or bashed by my new bessie, Nube!'

'How does he know so much about it?' Pig whispered to Wally.

'Magpiedia,' Wally explained. 'He's been on the Internet.'

'Nicely put, Thug.'
Jimmy gave him a
pat. His eyes glit-
tered. 'Now drink it.'
Thug dipped his
beak into the saucepan

and slurped up some of the mixture. 'Not bad!' he said. 'A bit like stewed worm.' He took another slurp. 'Could do with more salt though.'

'Can you feel any wisdom coming on?' Slasher asked.

'Not yet.' Thug polished off the mixture and sat back, waiting. He closed his eyes. Suddenly they pinged wide open. His feathers shook.

'Something's happening!' Jimmy said. 'Stand back!'

BOOOOOOOOOOOOOFFFFFFF!

Thug keeled over.

The other magpies stared.

'Oops,' said Wally.

Just then the caravan door opened.

'Vot are you doing?' Zenia screeched. 'Vy is that magpie orange?'

Thug's feathers had turned the colour of Ginger Biscuit's fur.

Zenia Klob prodded Thug with a skewer. 'And vy are its legs all hairy?' she demanded.

Thug's legs were covered in wiry ginger hair. Somehow the hair had got mixed up with the feathers on his bottom, or the other way around.

It looked as though Thug was wearing a hairy pair of orange feather pants. Or a feathery pair of orange hair pants.

'Vait a minute!' Zenia spied the notebook. 'Vot's this?!' She grabbed it and flicked it open. Her eyeballs popped. 'You tried to trick me, didn't you, you naughty birdies?' she shrieked. 'Thought you'd try to vork out how to get the lost treasure for yourselves vile Ginger and I veren't looking!' She reached for the hairpins. 'Traitors!' she screeched. 'Biscuit, you know vot to do.'

'GGGGGGRRRRRR!' Ginger Biscuit advanced on the magpies.

'Goodbye, cruel world,' Thug whispered. He held out his orange wings at full stretch. 'I'm coming, Nube! Prepare to receive the chosen one! I'm ready to embrace death!'

'We're not!' The other magpies fluttered backwards, squawking.

POP. POP. POP. POP. Ginger Biscuit popped out his claws one by one. He was going to enjoy this.

'Ah ha ha ha! Ah ha ha ha!' Suddenly a horrible screech rang round the room. It was Zenia, laughing. 'You pathetic pigeons!' she shrieked, holding the book up. 'You hopeless hens! You've got the wrong book! This isn't Howard Toffly's book of Ancient Egyptian visdom. It's Herman Tucker's build-a-beard-jumper manual. He vants to re-grow the one that Biscuit sliced! Ah ha ha ha. Ah ha ha ha!'

Suddenly the laughter switched off.

'Vich means unfortunately ve still need you. Change of plan, Biscuit. No magpie killing today.'

Ginger Biscuit looked disappointed.

Zenia Klob clicked the steel toes of her heavy boots. 'Go back to the island with them, my evil pet,' she addressed Ginger. 'And make sure they get the right book this time.'

Atticus was dreaming. In his dream he was sitting on a magnificent throne inside a beautiful golden temple, with Mimi by his side. Crowds of people lined the temple to worship him. The people tiptoed past Atticus one by one, bowing as they went and offering him gifts. Atticus waved a paw at each one to say thank you. Inspector Cheddar was next in line. He shuffled towards Atticus with a squeaky wheelie trolley, reached in and produced a fish pie bursting with prawns. But it wasn't really Inspector Cheddar. It was Zenia Klob in disguise! And the pie was full of magpies not prawns. They flew at him, chattering madly. At the same time a huge ginger cat leapt from the wheelie trolley ready to devour him . . .

'MYAAAAAAWWWWW!'

'Atticus!' Mimi was shaking him.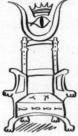
'Wake up. You're having a nightmare!'

Atticus looked about. He was lying on Inspector Cheddar's favourite armchair in the sitting room at number 2 Blossom Crescent. His paws were trembling.

'What's wrong?' Mimi asked gently.

'I don't know,' Atticus shook his head. 'I just feel . . . weird. I felt the same when I was at the crypt today. I didn't want to go, but when I got there I couldn't leave!'

'Is it something to do with Howard Toffly's book?' Mimi asked.

'Maybe,' Atticus admitted. 'It sounds stupid, but I feel like I have to protect it,' he said. 'It's almost as if it belongs to me!'

'It's not stupid.' Mimi gazed at him in silence for a moment. 'Aisha says that cats have a sixth sense,' she said eventually.

'What do you mean?'

'Well, most animals have five senses: smell, taste, touch, hearing and sight,' Mimi explained.

79

'But cats have another one: my owner Aisha says they remember things from their other lives. She calls it "instinct" – they just seem to know things without being taught.'

'That's exactly what I feel!' Atticus exclaimed. 'I know I have to protect that book. I have to stop the magpies and Biscuit stealing it. Which means I have to steal it myself. What should I do, Mimi? I don't want to be a cat burglar again.'

'Follow your instinct,' Mimi said. 'Protect the book. It's not stealing.' She squeezed his paw. 'If it really does belong to you.'

'But how could it?' Atticus asked, bewildered.

'I don't know,' Mimi said. 'Just do what you have to. We can't let Klob get her hands on it. And don't worry,' she reassured him, 'the kids and I will watch your tail.'

She waited until Atticus had fallen asleep again. Then she padded back into the kitchen and settled down in the basket. She decided she would check on him later, just to make sure he didn't have any more nightmares.

'What are you two doing out of bed?' Mrs Cheddar asked. 'It's three o'clock in the morning!'

Michael and Callie were standing in her bedroom doorway in their pyjamas. 'It's Atticus,' Michael said. 'He's gone.'

'Gone?' Mrs Cheddar rubbed her eyes. 'He's a cat. He goes out at night. He'll be all right.'

'No he won't, Mum,' Michael insisted. 'Mimi woke us. We can tell she's worried.'

Mimi jumped on to Mrs Cheddar's bed. 'Meow!' she yowled. Her golden eyes looked anxious. She put out a paw and touched Mrs Cheddar's hand.

'Maybe he went with Dad,' Mrs Cheddar suggested. 'To stake out the Home for Abandoned Cats.'

'I don't think so,' Michael said. 'Dad told him to stay here. He's taken him off the case. He thinks Atticus tipped off the kittens.'

'Well, where do you think Atticus is, then?' Mrs Cheddar struggled out of bed and put her dressing gown on.

'We think he's gone back to the crypt,' Callie gulped.

'*Back* to the crypt?!' Mrs Cheddar repeated.

'What are you talking about?'

Michael and Callie traded guilty looks.

'You tell her,' Callie said.

'Okay.' Michael took a deep breath. 'Don't be cross, Mum,' he said, 'but it's like this.' He explained what had happened that afternoon with Mr Tucker. 'The magpies took the wrong book.'

'Why didn't you tell me before?' Mrs Cheddar asked.

'Because Mr Tucker didn't want us to,' Callie explained. 'He thought Mrs Tucker would get mad with him if she found out what he'd been doing. But now Atticus has disappeared and it's our fault.' She was close to tears. 'He's gone back for Howard Toffly's book.'

'How can you be so sure?' Mrs Cheddar asked.

'Atticus didn't want to leave without it earlier.' Michael said. 'He was acting weird: like he wanted to stay and protect it from the magpies.'

Mimi began to purr.

'Is that where he is, Mimi? At the crypt?' Mrs Cheddar reached out and stroked her. Mimi arched her back. She purred harder. It wasn't anything like as loud as Atticus's throaty roar but Mrs

Cheddar got the idea anyway. 'We must tell Dad,' she said firmly. 'He needs to know the magpies are back. He needs to know the Tofflys have put Klob on to Howard Toffly's book.' Suddenly a thought struck her. 'I'll bet those villains are behind the graffiti knitting.' She reached for her mobile. 'I'll call him now.'

'There isn't time!' Callie said. 'And anyway, Dad won't believe you. He's convinced the kittens did it.'

Mrs Cheddar hesitated. 'All right,' she agreed. 'Get dressed. We'll go to Toffly Hall and get the Tuckers. Mrs Tucker will have to find out sooner or later about the laboratory. We'll tell Dad in the morning.'

🐾

'This is all your fault, Herman.'

A little while later, in the grounds of Toffly Hall, Mrs Cheddar, Mr and Mrs Tucker, Michael, Callie and Mimi crept along the path through the trees towards the lake. The moon was bright so the humans could just about make out where they were going, although the canopy of branches made everything dark and shadowy. Mimi had no problem: cats can see in the dark.

Mrs Tucker was cross. 'You should have told me what you were up to, you old roach!' she said.

'My fault?!' Mr Tucker spluttered. 'I ain't the one flying about stealing people's notebooks. It's them magpies youze should be complaining about.'

Mrs Tucker ignored him. 'Goodness knows what's going to happen now.' She shivered. 'I've had a bad feeling about this cat pharaoh business from the very beginning.'

'Atticus?' Mrs Cheddar called. 'Atticus!'

'He can't have gone faaarrr!' Mr Tucker grumbled. His wooden leg kept getting stuck down rabbit holes. 'I mean, he can't row a boat, and he's not going to swim to the island, is he? He hates water.'

'You sure about that, Herman?' Mrs Tucker snapped. 'Atticus seems to be able to do most things.'

They reached the lake. It was black, like ink.

There was no sign of Atticus.

'Now what do we do?' Mrs Cheddar said.

Mrs Tucker pulled out a pair of night-vision binoculars from her basket. She peered through them.

'I knew it!' she whispered. She handed them to Michael.

Michael gasped. There, in the middle of the lake, crouched on a log, was Atticus. He was paddling towards the island with his front paws.

'Let me see!' Callie grabbed the binoculars.

It was Mrs Cheddar's turn after that. Then Mr Tucker's.

'Will you look at that!' he whistled. 'Youze got to admit, that cat's got claaasss. He can crew me boat any day.'

'Come on,' Mrs Tucker said. 'He's going to need some help if those magpies come back. Especially if Klob and Biscuit are with them.'

They jumped into the rowing boat. Mr Tucker clambered in after them and took the oars. Soon they were skimming swiftly across the lake.

They landed at the jetty.

Wet paw prints on the wooden planks told them Atticus was just ahead.

'Atticus!' Callie hissed. 'Atticus!'

'It's no good,' said Mrs Tucker. 'He can't hear you. And even if he could, I'm not sure he'd listen.'

They hurried along the mossy path to the crypt. Mr Tucker led the way with the torch. He parted the branches to reveal Howard Toffly's burial place.

'Holy coley!' Mrs Tucker breathed when she saw the pyramid.

Mr Tucker pushed open the door. 'Wait, while I get me generator working,' he said.

POOOOOOOFFF!

Light flooded the laboratory.

Mrs Tucker let out a snort of disapproval when she saw Mr Tucker's experiments.

'Look!' Michael cried.

The padlock to the second chamber lay on the floor where Atticus had picked it open with his claws. The door creaked on its rusty hinges.

'Come on!'

'What about the curse?' Callie whispered.

'If Atticus isn't worried about it then neither am I,' Michael said bravely. He grabbed the torch and made for the door.

'Nor me!' Callie followed him. She crossed her

fingers behind her back.

'Me neither!' Mrs Cheddar said a little prayer. She scooped up Mimi.

'This is the best fun I've had since me beard-jumper got chopped.' Mr Tucker collected some more torches from his supplies and clanked after them. 'Sorry about the experiments, Edna,' he added. 'Are youze coming?'

'Bring it on!' Mrs Tucker swung her basket. 'If that cat pharaoh does anything to Atticus, he'll have me to answer to. Besides, I won't let Klob get her hands on that book. Let's go.'

9

'Howard Toffly's coffin,' Michael whispered.

They were in a second chamber, bigger and cooler than the one Mr Tucker was using as his laboratory. In the middle an oblong marble coffin stood on a platform. Screwed into it was a gold plaque.

The group tiptoed towards it. Michael flashed his torch at the plaque.

HOWARD MACKINTOSH TOFFLY
1879–1934
MAY HE FINALLY BE AT PEACE

'It's like a fridge in here.' Callie shivered.

'That's so his corpse doesn't decompose,' Mr Tucker said helpfully.

CRASH!

A gust of wind blew the door shut. The only light came from the thin beams of their torches.

Callie screamed.

'It's okay, darling!' Mrs Cheddar held her hand.

They flashed their torches around.

There was no sign of Atticus.

'He must be here somewhere,' Mrs Cheddar said, her voice shaking.

The children felt their way around the walls. 'Atticus!' they whispered. 'Atticus!'

'What about down here?' Mrs Tucker said.

In one corner of the room was a trapdoor. Someone had lifted it up. Steep steps led down from it into the dark earth.

'Atticus couldn't lift that.' Mrs Cheddar frowned.

'If he can paddle across a lake, he can lift a trapdoor,' Mrs Tucker said. 'I reckon he's sleepwalking. And when you're sleepwalking, you can do pretty much anything your brain tells you to. Come on.' She put Mimi in her basket and led the way carefully down the narrow steps. Michael came next with the torch. Mrs Cheddar followed with Callie. Mr Tucker limped along at the rear, cursing his wooden leg.

'There he is!' Callie cried.

Atticus was a little way ahead of them, padding slowly down the steps into the darkness.

'Atticus!' Michael whispered.

'Atticus!' Callie said it louder. Her voice echoed off the damp walls.

Atticus didn't seem to hear them. He padded on.

'Shhhh,' Mrs Tucker said. 'If he's sleepwalking we need to be careful how we wake him up.'

'Why?' Callie hissed.

'In case he gets stuck in his dream,' Mrs Tucker whispered grimly.

The steps ended in a passageway. Atticus padded along it. Suddenly he stopped. He'd reached a brick wall.

'It's a dead end!' Michael sounded half relieved, half disappointed.

'Wait!' Callie breathed. 'What's he doing now?'

'He's looking for something!' Mrs Cheddar said.

Atticus paced up and down, his eyes fixed to the wall. Eventually he found what he was looking for. He raised a paw. He placed it against a brick. There was a grinding sound as part of the wall rolled sideways.

90

'The secret chamber!' Callie whispered.

Atticus disappeared through the opening.

The others followed a safe distance behind. They paused to gaze at the wall in the torchlight. It was covered in strange symbols.

'Hieroglyphs!' Mrs Cheddar whispered.

There were paintings too.

'The cat pharaoh!' Mrs Tucker gasped.

The paintings were of a large black-and-brown-striped tabby with white socks and deep green eyes. He was wearing a pharaoh's headdress of blue and gold.

'It's Atticus!' Michael and Callie said together.

'Flamin' fishfingers!' Mr Tucker whistled.

'It looks just like him!' Mrs Cheddar stared.

'I knew it!' Mrs Tucker muttered.

They entered the secret chamber. The floor was littered with statues of the cat pharaoh. They looked identical to the paintings outside.

'They can't all be real,' Mrs Cheddar said.

'They're not.' Mrs Tucker picked one up and examined it.

'How do *you* know, Edna?' Mr Tucker asked, bewildered.

'Because when I was Agent Whelk, I spent several months in Egypt living with the Bedouin in the desert,' Mrs Tucker said. 'I've been to the pyramids. I've seen Ancient Egyptian treasure. These are fake.'

'So where's the book?' Michael whispered.

'I'll bet one of these is a *real* statue Howard Toffly stole from the lost city of Nebu-Mau.' Mrs Tucker looked round slowly. 'He's tried to disguise it by having all these replicas made. My guess is the book will be hidden inside the real one.' She pointed at Atticus. 'If anyone can find it, he can.'

Atticus picked his way amongst the statues. He stopped at one and sniffed. He circled it for moment then kicked the others out of the way with his hind legs.

'He's got it!' Mrs Tucker said.

Atticus looked keenly at the statue. He raised a paw and popped out his claws. He reached towards it and tinkered with one of the ears.

The statue sprang apart.

Atticus felt inside and pulled out an old leather-bound book.

Suddenly there was a loud moan from somewhere up above.

'MYAAAAAWWWW!'

'What was that?' Callie looked round.

'It's Biscuit!' Mrs Cheddar cried.

'Chaka-chaka-chaka-chaka-chaka!'

'And those mangy magpies!' Mr Tucker shouted.

'Quick! Mimi! Get Atticus!' Mrs Tucker ordered.

Mimi leapt out of the basket.

'Be careful!' Mrs Tucker warned. 'He's still in a trance.'

The beat of wings grew louder. There was a rush of air as the magpies swooped into the secret chamber behind them.

'Chaka-chaka-chaka-chaka-chaka!' An orange one with hairy legs flew at Mr Tucker.

'You're the beast that stole me notebook!' Mr Tucker swiped at Thug.

'Atticus!' Mimi hissed. 'Wake up!' She touched him on the shoulder.

Atticus jumped. 'Mimi?' He looked round in surprise. 'Where am I?'

'You mean you don't know?' Mimi said.

'I . . .'

'MYYAAAAWWWW!'

'Biscuit!' Atticus cried. He snatched up the book

in his teeth.

Mr Tucker scooped Atticus and Mimi up in his arms. 'Come on, youze twooze,' he said. 'There's no time to lose.'

'Chaka-chaka-chaka-chaka-chaka!'

Mrs Tucker was fighting the magpies off with her basket.

Mrs Cheddar, Callie and Michael hurled fake statues at Ginger Biscuit.

SMASH! SMASH! SMASH!

The statues shattered against the walls and floor.

Biscuit turned and twisted, hissing and spitting like an old kettle. He was cornered.

'Retreat!' Mr Tucker roared.

They hurried back up the steps.

'Somebody close the trapdoor!' Mr Tucker yelled. 'I've got me arms full of cats.'

BANG!

Mrs Tucker slammed it shut.

THUD!

The trapdoor juddered as something heavy smashed into it from below.

'Biscuit!' Mrs Cheddar screamed. 'Come on. It won't hold him for long!'

'MMYYYAAAWWWW!'

They raced back past Howard Toffly's coffin.

CRASH! Mrs Tucker pushed the door to the tomb shut. She braced herself against it. 'Get the padlock!'

CRUNCH!

Biscuit bashed into the door from the other side.

Mrs Tucker staggered.

CLICK!

Mrs Cheddar locked the padlock. 'That'll keep him busy for a while!'

'MMYYYAAAWWWW!'

They ran out into the night towards the jetty.

'Get into the boat!' Mrs Tucker puffed. 'Klob won't be far away.'

They cast off. Mr Tucker grabbed the oars and steered them out into the lake. Just then they heard the chug of a motorboat.

'Is that her?' Michael whispered.

Callie's face was white with fear.

'Now what do we do?' Mrs Cheddar held the kids' hands tight.

'Leave this to me!' Mrs Tucker told her. 'We've got the book, Klob!' she shouted.

Chug, chug, chug.

'If you come any closer we'll chuck it in the lake.'

The chugging stopped.

'And your evil animal pals need some help,' Mrs Tucker yelled. 'We've locked them in the crypt.'

There was silence.

'And don't even think about hairpinning me!' Mrs Tucker took the book from Atticus's clenched teeth and held it over the water. 'Or I'll drop this in the drink.'

'I'll get you for this, Velk!' a voice screeched through the darkness. 'Just you vait!'

The chugging started up again and faded away.

'She's gone!' Callie whispered. 'Are you all right, Atticus?'

Atticus was trembling violently. Both his ears drooped. Callie picked him up and cuddled him. She buried her face in his fur. Michael tickled his chin.

Atticus began to purr weakly.

'He's feeling better, thank goodness,' Mrs Cheddar said. She found a cat treat in her pocket and offered it to him.

Atticus took it gratefully. He was starving.

Mrs Tucker wrapped the book in her cardigan and placed it carefully in the basket. 'Now let's get you home,' she said, giving Atticus a sardine. 'Before you get yourself into any more trouble.'

'I don't have time for all this!'

The next morning, in the kitchen at number 2
Blossom Crescent, Mrs Cheddar and the kids were
telling Inspector Cheddar about their adventures
of the previous night.

It wasn't going too well.

'But, Dad!' Callie shouted. 'The magpies were
there. And Biscuit. They were after Howard
Toffly's book.'

'The first time around they stole Mr Tucker's
beard-jumper experiment notebook by mistake,'
Michael explained. 'That's why one of the magpies
was orange.'

'Orange,' Inspector Cheddar repeated sarcasti-
cally. 'I see.'

'Atticus knew they'd come back,' Callie insisted. 'And he knew where the real book was hidden.'

'And he looks exactly like the cat pharaoh!' Michael told him. 'It was amazing, Dad. You should have seen him! He worked out how to open the secret chamber. He can read hieroglyphs.'

Inspector Cheddar snorted. 'I have never heard such a load of old rubbish in my life!' he said.

'Darling, it's true!' Mrs Cheddar protested. 'We did see the magpies. And Biscuit. And we heard Klob. The kids are right: Atticus rescued the book. Mrs Tucker has it.'

Inspector Cheddar sighed. *Orange magpies! Secret chambers! Cats reading hieroglyphs!* What nonsense! He glanced at Atticus, who was snoozing in his basket, curled up next to Mimi. Inspector Cheddar couldn't help thinking how straightforward his life had been before Atticus Grammaticus Cattypuss

Claw turned up on the doorstep.

'You didn't see anything,' he said crossly. 'It was your imagination playing tricks in the dark. And even if Atticus did find a book, it's not going to tell you the way to the golden city of cats. There's no such thing.' He chortled. 'Next you'll be telling me that Atticus is descended from the cat pharaoh and it's his destiny to protect the lost city of Nebu-Mau from being discovered by the Tofflys.'

The kids clapped their hands.

'That's brilliant, Dad!' Michael shouted.

'Great thinking!' Callie's eyes shone.

'Darling, you are clever!' Mrs Cheddar agreed.

'I was joking!' Inspector Cheddar thundered. He shook his head. 'I can't listen to any more of this. I've got important knitting crimes to solve.' He snatched up his cap and strode out.

'I suppose there's no point in telling him who the graffiti knitters really are?' Callie sighed.

'I don't think so,' Mrs Cheddar said heavily. 'Not until we have proof.'

Just then the phone rang.

Mrs Cheddar picked it up.

'Okay . . . yes . . . that's great . . . I'll ring the office and tell them I can't go in today . . . we'll meet you at the train station . . . I'll get Atticus and Mimi up now.'

'Who was that?' Michael asked.

'It was Mrs Tucker.' Mrs Cheddar grinned. 'She's made an appointment to see Professor Verry-Clever at the British Museum in London. She wants us to bring Atticus.'

🐾

Atticus knew London well from his years as a cat burglar, but he'd never been to the British Museum before. The taxi dropped them at the gates. Atticus and Mimi hurried after the humans into a courtyard. They scurried up the steps into the museum.

Professor Verry-Clever met them at the door.

'This way,' he said. He led them through the museum.

Atticus caught a fleeting glimpse of rooms full of huge stone statues.

Soon they arrived at the Professor's office. 'Don't mind Cleopatra,' he said, opening the door.

'Who's Cleopatra?' Callie asked.

'She's my mummy!' Edmund Verry-Clever's eyes twinkled. 'She was a gift from the University of Cairo.'

A painted sarcophagus stood upright in the corner next to a statue of a sphinx. It was in the shape of a woman. She had a beautiful painted face with huge almond eyes and dark eyebrows. Her clothes were gold and red and aqua blue.

Atticus squinted at it. The colours reminded him of something from a long time ago.

'Can we see inside it?' Michael begged.

'All right.' The Professor clicked a catch. Carefully he pulled the sarcophagus open.

'Eeerrrrggghh!' Callie cried in disgust.

Mimi flinched.

Atticus felt only curiosity. The figure inside the sarcophagus was swathed in dusty brown bandages from head to toe. Again, he felt he'd seen something like it before, but he couldn't remember where. He tiptoed forward to take a closer look. Then he froze. He could have sworn the mummy moved! He rubbed his eyes with his paw.

'Not so pretty in the flesh, is she?' The Professor said gleefully. 'But you've got to remember Cleopatra is about four thousand years old.' He closed the sarcophagus.

'What are those?' Michael pointed to a display cabinet beside Cleopatra. Inside was a cruel-looking statue of a bird with black glittering eyes. Balanced on its head was a red disc. It stood over the bodies of two other birds that lay beneath it, wings out, beaks gaping.

'That's Horus, the Egyptian God of the Sky. It's a sacrifice to Osiris, the God of the Dead, who was believed to be Horus's father.'

Atticus turned away. The statue reminded him of Jimmy Magpie.

'Now let's get down to business,' Professor Verry-Clever said.

'We found this in Howard Toffly's crypt.' Mrs Tucker unravelled the leather-bound book from her cardigan and handed it to him. 'Well, that is to say, Atticus did.' She told the Professor what had happened the night before.

Atticus listened, spellbound. *He did all that?* He supposed he must have, if Mrs Tucker said he did. The scary thing was, he couldn't remember any of it, until the bit where Mimi woke him up and they were fighting off Biscuit and the magpies.

Edmund Verry-Clever listened in silence, occasionally casting curious looks in Atticus's direction. 'Remarkable,' he said when she'd finished. 'Quite remarkable.' He took out a magnifying glass from his desk, pulled on a pair of cotton gloves and opened the book.

'Hieroglyphs!' he breathed.  'From the Eleventh Dynasty.' The way he said it, it was as if someone had just told him he'd won the lottery. 'This is the most exciting discovery

I have *ever* witnessed,' he said. His brow knotted in a frown of concentration.

'Can you read them?' Michael asked.

Professor Verry-Clever nodded slowly. 'I can understand most of them. They tell the way to the lost city of Nebu-Mau: the golden city of cats.'

'So Howard Toffly did find the city!' Mrs Cheddar gripped the edge of the desk.

'Yes, he must have stumbled across the city by chance,' the Professor said solemnly, 'entered the cat pharaoh's tomb and made off with the book and the statue that Atticus found in the crypt. That's why he was cursed.' He looked dreamy. 'This book gives us the chance to follow in his footsteps.'

'Does it say how to get there?' Mr Tucker asked. 'Only we could go in me boat if youze like!' he offered generously.

'Don't be silly, Herman!' Mrs Tucker snapped. 'Nebu-Mau's in the desert.'

The Professor scrutinised the symbols. 'According to the hieroglyphs,' he said, 'the path to Nebu-Mau lies through sand *and* water.'

'How is that possible?' Mrs Cheddar whispered.

'I don't know.' Edmund Verry-Clever turned a page. 'But I see the desert and the parting of water. I see palm trees and sand dunes. I see a city of temples and pyramids. I see treasure beyond the dreams of men.'

Atticus jumped on the desk. He wanted to see too. Fragments of the previous night were coming back to him. Nebu-Mau sounded like the place he'd read about on the wall of the secret chamber in Howard Toffly's crypt.

'I see a prosperous place full of rich and beautiful cats,' the Professor said. 'I see people gathering there from far and wide bringing wonderful gifts.'

Atticus's eyes followed the hieroglyphs. It was easy-peasy-cat-paw-squeezy to read them. He waited politely for the Professor to finish deciphering them then turned the page with his paw.

'I see a temple and a palace,' the Professor continued. He had one eye on Atticus. 'They belong to a great ruler: a wise and mighty tabby cat with white paws. It is he the people have come to worship.'

Atticus started to purr. That was exactly what Atticus saw too! He was glad Professor Verry-Clever was so brainy. For some reason, the rest of the humans didn't seem to have a clue what the hieroglyphs meant. Nor did Mimi. They were looking at him and the Professor in complete puzzlement. Atticus couldn't understand what the problem was: normally they were pretty good at reading.

'Who is the great ruler?' Michael demanded.

Edmund Verry-Clever looked up. 'He is the cat pharaoh: Cattypuss the Great.'

'Cattypuss!' Mrs Tucker shrieked. 'That's Atticus's middle name. Well, one of them.'

'Bloomin' hake!' Mr Tucker exclaimed.

'Any idea how he got it?' the Professor demanded sharply.

'No,' Mrs Cheddar shook her head. 'He just arrived on the doorstep with it.'

Atticus touched his neckerchief. His name was sewn on it in spidery writing.

ATTICUS GRAMMATICUS CATTYPUSS CLAW

He'd never thought about his name before. Or where it had come from. It had just been there, around his neck, since he was a kitten.

The Professor eyed Atticus with growing respect. He offered Atticus the book. Atticus turned to the final page. He had a feeling this would be the best bit of the story.

'Only the true descendant of Cattypuss the Great can open the tomb of the cat pharaoh,' the Professor read. 'It is only he who has the necessary wisdom, passed down from previous lives. It is only he who may enter the tomb without being cursed.'

I knew that! Atticus thought proudly. 'Instinct' Mimi called it. And he had it in bucket-loads. He looked round. Everyone was staring at him, including Mimi. He wondered why.

The humans all started talking at once.

In the din Atticus caught the words

– 'Egypt' and

– 'expedition' and

– 'top secret' and

– 'dangerous' and

– 'Dad was right' and

– 'Klob' and

– 'Biscuit' and

– 'magpies' and

– 'Lord and Lady Toffly' and

– 'over my dead body' (several times from Mrs Tucker)

– and his own name repeated over and over and over again:

Atticus, Cattypuss,

Atticus, Cattypuss,

Atticus, Cattypuss.

Until Atticus felt quite dizzy. He had to squeeze Mimi's paw to keep himself from falling off the desk.

Eventually Edmund Verry-Clever raised his hand for silence. 'So we are agreed. We will mount an expedition to Egypt to rediscover the lost city of Nebu-Mau: the golden city of cats. Atticus will lead us. In the meantime I will keep the book safe here in the museum's vault while the necessary arrangements are made. You will keep Atticus safe at home. We will leave in two days' time.'

Everyone else nodded.

Atticus felt puzzled. Of course he'd be happy to go to Egypt. It was hot there and he liked sunbathing. But lead an expedition to rediscover the lost city of Nebu-Mau? That sounded like hard work. And there was the curse to think about. And why did they need to keep him safe? He could look after himself. 'Why me?' he whispered to Mimi. 'Can't someone else do it?

'It has to be you, Atticus,' Mimi purred quietly. 'Don't you see? That's how you can read the hieroglyphs. That's how you knew where to find the book.'

'What do you mean?' Atticus said, puzzled.

'Oh, Atticus,' Mimi cried. 'Wake up! The book's talking about you! *You* are the descendant of Cattypuss the Great.'

'Remarkable, quite remarkable!'

When his visitors had gone, Professor Edmund Verry-Clever sat poring over the book. He would lock it in the museum's vault later. Right now, he just wanted to admire it. It was the most wonderful object he had ever encountered in all the years he had spent studying Ancient Egypt. Imagine! To discover the lost city of Nebu-Mau; to find the golden city of cats; to enter the tomb of cat pharaoh, Cattypuss the Great: it was every scholar's dream.

The Professor couldn't believe his good fortune. What a stroke of luck to come across a tabby who was descended from Cattypuss the Great himself! Atticus would lead them to the city, just as he had led his family to the stolen book in the crypt. It was fate. It was a miracle. It was the will of the Ancient Egyptian gods. And you couldn't argue with them, unless you wanted to die a horrible death, like Howard Toffly.

TAP. TAP. TAP.

The Professor looked up.

TAP. TAP. TAP.

He frowned. The noise seemed to be coming from the glass display case of Horus. He got up to investigate.

TAP. TAP. TAP.

The Professor froze.

Horus had moved. He was staring up at him with glittering eyes, tapping at the glass. And the two sacrificial birds weren't dead any more. They were hopping about chattering at one another.

The professor staggered backwards.

KNOCK! KNOCK! KNOCK!

He turned his head in disbelief.

KNOCK! KNOCK! KNOCK!

The knocking was coming from inside the sarcophagus.

He watched in horror as the door swung open.

The mummy stepped out, arms outstretched. It reached under the wrappings covering its head. Something sharp gleamed in its bandaged hand.

The Professor screamed.

ZIP!

A hairpin flew through the air. It hit the Professor in the chest. He folded to the floor.

'MMYYAAAAWWWWWW!'

The last thing he remembered before he passed out was a furry flash of ginger as the sphinx came to life.

🐾

'Good vork!' Zenia Klob prodded the Professor with her bandaged boot. 'Now get him in the trolley. Qvick! Before somebody comes.'

Ginger Biscuit got the squeaky wheelie trolley out of the cupboard and heaved Edmund Verry-Clever into it. He flicked out his claws one by one – POP. POP. POP. POP. – and released the three birds from the glass case.

'Ve'll take this!' Zenia grabbed Howard Toffly's

stolen book off the desk and pressed it to her bandaged lips. 'And the Professor. That vay ve von't be followed. No vun else knows vere the lost city is. All ve need now is Atticus.'

'Chaka-chaka-chaka-chaka!' the magpies chattered angrily.

'Grrrrrr,' Biscuit growled.

'Silence!' She clicked her boots. 'I don't care vether you like it or not,' she hissed. 'Ve need Atticus to get the treasure. He is the only vun who can open the tomb.' She glanced out of the window. The Tofflys were perched on the domed roof with several bin bags full of wool, some knitting needles and a vat of Thumpers' Knitquick. Pig, Gizzard and Wally hovered nearby. Zenia raised a fist. 'Let's go and get him,' she said, 'vile the Tofflys do the vest.'

At about four o'clock that afternoon the call came through to the Chief Inspector of Bigsworth that the graffiti knitters had struck London. The British Museum had been cocooned in a mohair vest. The Chief Inspector set off for Scotland Yard.

'Get Cheddar!' he yelled at his secretary on the way out. 'Tell him he's an idiot. I was right all along. It's not Smellie. Tell him the Police Commissioner wants to see us. NOW!'

Inspector Cheddar was sitting in his wife's car opposite the Home for Abandoned Cats eating a Twix when the secretary got hold of him on his walkie-talkie.

He could hardly believe his ears. *Not Smellie! Then who?* Inspector Cheddar set off for Scotland Yard, his jaw set. Something told him this was going to be BIG. VERY BIG!

NEE NAW NEE NAW NEE NAW!

This was a job for the professionals. He zoomed up the motorway, whizzed through the streets of London, skidded to a halt outside Scotland Yard and raced into the building.

The Police Commissioner was waiting for him in his office.

'Ah, Cheddar, there you are,' the Police Commissioner said. 'Good to see you again.' (They had worked together on the Crown Jewels case with Atticus.) He shook his head. 'Bad business this.'

'Yes, sir,' Inspector Cheddar said. 'Knitting crime is no joke.'

'He's not talking about *that*, Cheddar!' the Chief Inspector of Bigsworth roared. 'The knitting's just a cover-up.'

Inspector Cheddar giggled. 'Good one, sir!'

'Are you all right, Cheddar?' the Police Commissioner frowned.

'Yes, sir.' Inspector Cheddar coughed. Being in the company of the Police Commissioner always seemed to make him nervous.

'We had a call from Agent Whelk,' the Commissioner told him. 'Known to you as Mrs Edna Tucker. She explained about Howard Toffly and the book he stole when he was in Egypt.'

Inspector Cheddar guffawed. 'I suppose she also told you that Atticus is descended from the cat pharaoh and that it's his destiny to protect the lost city of Nebu-Mau from being discovered by the Tofflys?'

'Something like that.' The Commissioner nodded seriously. 'Agent Whelk and your family had a meeting today at the British Museum with

Professor Verry-Clever at which Atticus was present. The Professor confirmed that the book is genuine. It seems that Atticus is a descendant of the cat pharaoh, Cattypuss the Great. Only Atticus can lead an expedition to find the lost city. He alone can defeat the curse.'

'Shut up!' Inspector Cheddar laughed.

'I beg your pardon?' the Police Commissioner looked astonished.

Inspector Cheddar saw he had made a mistake. 'I'm sorry, sir,' he said quickly, 'I didn't mean shut up as in "be quiet", I meant shut up as in "no way". Are you sure?'

'Oh, I see . . . well . . . yes way,' the Police Commissioner replied. 'It's true. The problem is we aren't the only people who know about the book. Our old enemies Klob, Biscuit and the magpies are back. They've teamed up with the Tofflys. We think they're behind the knitting crimes. It was just a diversion to put the police off the scent while they went after the book.'

Inspector Cheddar looked sheepish. That was exactly what his family had told him. He really must remember to listen to them next time.

'I knew it!' the Chief Inspector of Bigsworth lied.

'When we finally unpicked our way into the museum,' the Police Commissioner said sombrely, 'we found that Professor Verry-Clever had gone missing,' the Commissioner went on. 'So had the book. We think Klob and her gang must have followed Agent Whelk into the museum, kidnapped the Professor and taken the book. We think they'll try and use the Professor to decipher the hieroglyphs. But from what Agent Whelk tells us, without Atticus they won't be able to open the tomb. Or if they do, they'll regret it. Fortunately they don't know that. They're probably on their way to Egypt already.'

'What do you want me to do, sir?' Inspector Cheddar asked. He wasn't laughing now.

'You're going to Cairo, as planned,' the Commissioner said, 'with your family, Agent Whelk and her husband. And Atticus, of course. Your mission, together with Police Cat Sergeant Claw, is to find the lost city of Nebu-Mau, rescue Edmund Verry-Clever, recover the book, capture the villains and alert the Egyptian government to the whereabouts of the treasure.'

'Without being cursed by the cat pharaoh,' the Chief Inspector of Bigsworth added cheerfully.

'Quite so. Think you can manage that, Cheddar?' the Commissioner asked.

'Leave it to me, sir!' Inspector Cheddar said. 'You can rest assured: nothing will go wrong while I'm in charge.'

1·2

'Chaka-chaka-chaka-chaka-chaka!'

That night the magpies gathered in the garden at number 2 Blossom Crescent.

Ginger Biscuit slouched in the shadows.

'Claw's basket's by the fridge,' Jimmy said. 'I remember it from the last time we were here.'

'Maybe they've got him a special pharaoh bed,' Thug sighed. 'Lucky thing! I wish I was related to royalty. I've always fancied being a magpie prince of Egypt.'

'GGGRRRRRRRRR,' Ginger Biscuit growled.

'Someone's in a bad mood!' Thug nudged Slasher. Since their discovery at the British Museum that Atticus was related to Cattypuss the Great they'd found a brilliant new way to wind Biscuit up.

'Imagine Claw being descended from a cat pharaoh,' Slasher said loudly. He winked at Thug. 'That makes him well posh.'

'Yeah, fancy that!' Thug cawed. 'I wonder if he's got any priceless headdresses tucked away.'

'GGGRRRRRRR!'

'Bound to have!' Slasher agreed. 'And some nice amulets too.'

'What's a hamulet?' Thug asked.

'It's a type of old bracelet,' Slasher explained. 'The type that costs a lot of money.'

'That makes him richer than you, Ginger, right?' Thug hooted.

'As well as posher,' Slasher cawed.

'SHUT IT!' Ginger Biscuit leapt out of the shadows and swiped at them.

The magpies fluttered away.

'Temper, temper,' Thug said.

POP. POP. POP. POP. Biscuit popped out his claws and ripped at a sack of compost. Soil spilled from the slits. 'I'll kill Claw if it's the last thing I do!' he snarled.

'Cool it! You can't kill him yet. We need him. You heard what Klob said.' Jimmy Magpie's

122

eyes glittered. 'We've got a job to do. Get the sack.'

Thug and Slasher heaved something out of the bushes.

'You got the hairpin, Boss?'

'Yeah.' Jimmy unclipped a small cylinder from his leg. It contained one of Zenia's hairpins, generously coated on the points with sleeping potion.

'Let's get him.'

'I'll join you in a minute,' Biscuit snarled, 'when I've killed a few rats. It'll make me feel better.'

'I'll keep a look-out.' Jimmy passed the poisoned hairpin to Slasher. He fluttered up into a tree.

'Looks like we're doing all the work as usual!' Thug and Slasher hopped awkwardly through the cat flap with the sack. The house was pitch black and silent. Everyone was in bed. The two magpies peered at the basket.

They could see the shape of a cat. It was sleeping peacefully.

'Hurry up, Slash, before Claw wakes up.'

'Okay, okay.' Slasher held out the cylinder.

Silently, Thug removed the hairpin with his beak.

PRICK! He jabbed it at the cat's flank.

They heard a sigh, then deep rhythmic breathing.

'He's out like a light.'

The magpies unravelled the sack. They wriggled it over the cat's sleeping form.

Ginger Biscuit appeared through the cat flap. He picked the sack up with a growl, threw it across his shoulder and sauntered back across the kitchen floor and out into the night.

'Like taking worms from a baby robin!' Thug whispered, once they were outside.

'Hurry up,' Jimmy ordered. 'We don't want to miss the plane.'

The magpies flew off back to the caravan park.

Biscuit padded on with the sack on his back.

Zenia met him at the corner of Blossom Crescent. She was wearing her street-sweeper disguise. 'Good vork, Biscuit! In a few hours' time, 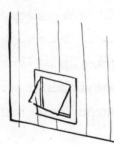 ve vill be in Egypt. And a few days after that ve vill be rich!' She put the sack in the squeaky dustcart.

'GGGRRRRR!' Biscuit threw a longing glance at the dustcart.

'Don't vorry, my cat-killing angel of darkness,' Zenia said. 'As soon as ve get the treasure, he's all yours. I promise. You can make as much mess as you like. There'll be plenty of sand vere ve're going to mop up the blood.'

Squeak . . . squeak . . . squeak!

Atticus woke up with a start. It was a sound he'd recognise anywhere. *Zenia?!* She was on her way to Egypt, wasn't she?

Squeak . . . squeak . . . squeak!

The sound came again.

Atticus leapt off the sofa, trying to shake the sleep out of his eyes. *Why had she come for him?* His heart was pounding. *She already had Professor Verry-Clever and the book. She didn't know she needed him as well.* Suddenly Atticus felt wide awake. His green eyes glowed. *OR DID SHE?* With a start he remembered Cleopatra, the mummy at the museum. *He'd thought he'd seen it move!* And the sacrifice to Horus! *Three birds. One of them looked a bit like Jimmy. He'd been so busy listening to Professor Verry-Clever, he hadn't given them a second thought. Until now.*

Atticus's mind was racing. Zenia could have disguised Jimmy, Thug and Slasher as the sacrifice and hidden herself in Cleopatra's sarcophagus! And the sphinx! *What if it was Biscuit?* It could have been. It had the same mean face and pumped-up body. *How could he have been so blind?* If it *was* them, they would have heard everything that was said. Atticus had been so caught up in reading the hiero-glyphs, he'd forgotten that Zenia Klob was a mistress of disguise.

Squeak . . . squeak . . . squeak.

Atticus stood behind the sitting-room door, his fur bristling. Biscuit wanted to kill him. Even Zenia might not be able to stop him this time. He pushed at the door tentatively with his paw. It moved freely. He would slam it in Ginger's face and knock him out, then run upstairs and get Inspector Cheddar. Maybe, if he moved fast, they wouldn't have to go to Egypt at all. They could capture Biscuit and Klob tonight.

Squeak . . . squeak . . . squeak.

Wait a minute! Atticus's ears pricked up. The sound was getting quieter, not louder. *Zenia was walking away.*

Very soon it disappeared altogether.

Atticus wriggled his eyebrows. He couldn't understand it. *What was going on? Unless . . .*

'Mimi!' he cried.

He raced into the kitchen.

'Mimi!'

At the sight of the empty basket he stopped dead.

'Oh no.'

His ears drooped.

'This is all my fault.'

Atticus took a deep breath. His whiskers twitched. He flexed his claws. *They wanted him: they'd get him. But not in the way they imagined.* 'I'll rescue you, Mimi,' he whispered. 'No matter what.'

Part Two
In Egypt

Atticus was hot. He was tired, thirsty and his whiskers were full of sand. He was also feeling slightly sick. The camel swayed from side to side like a boat.

'You all right, Atticus?' Mrs Tucker sat behind him on the camel. She wore a white robe with a purple veil. She seemed completely at home. 'Don't worry. Most people feel a bit sick on a camel to start with. You'll soon get used to it.'

Atticus purred faintly.

They were at the head of the procession, which consisted of a train of camels looping through the sand dunes into the heart of the desert. Behind them rode Callie and Michael, with Mrs Cheddar next to them. After them came Inspector Cheddar. Bringing up the rear was a very hot and cross Mr Tucker.

Atticus heard a bump behind him followed by a loud cry.

'Oh dear,' Mrs Tucker sighed, 'Herman's fallen off his camel again.'

The procession stopped.

'For cod's sake!' Mr Tucker roared. 'I can't get the hang of ridin' this thing. It's as bumpy as a baaarrrge in a sea swell. Me wooden leg keeps slippin'.'

'Stop complaining, Herman,' Mrs Tucker shouted. 'And hurry up and get back on. We'll never catch Klob at this rate.'

'I's doin' me best!' Mr Tucker grumbled. 'But I feel like a fish out of water. I miss the sea.'

'Why don't you *pretend* you're at sea?' Michael suggested. 'The camel feels a bit like a boat anyway the way it rocks from side to side.'

'Good thinking,' Mrs Tucker agreed. 'Camels are nicknamed ships of the desert, you know. Just pretend it is one, Herman, and you'll be fine.'

'Well, why didn't you say so before!' Mr Tucker said more cheerfully. The camel knelt down. Mr Tucker threw his wooden leg over the saddle and gripped on while the camel got jerkily to its feet.

'I name this ship *The Crafty Camel*,' he said giving the camel a slap on the backside. The camel cantered off. 'I think I's gettin' me sea legs!' Mr Tucker lurched to and fro across the sand.

Michael and Callie both giggled.

Another time Atticus would have thought it was funny too. But they were two days into the expedition and there was still no sign of Klob and her gang. Or, more importantly, of Mimi and Professor Verry-Clever.

'Are you sure we're going the right way?' Mrs Cheddar asked anxiously. All the humans had to go on were Howard Toffly's old maps from the library at Toffly Hall.

'Well?' Mrs Tucker looked at Atticus. 'Are we?' she said gently.

Atticus purred as loudly as his parched throat would allow. Although he didn't know exactly where they were going, he knew they were heading in the right direction. He could feel it in his fur.

'How can he tell?' Callie whispered in awe.

'It's his instinct,' Mrs Tucker explained. 'Because he's a descendant of Cattypuss the Great, part of him remembers.'

Atticus listened intently. That's what Mimi had said. He supposed it must be true. He had never been to Egypt in his present life, although he'd travelled to many other countries around the world during his career as a cat burglar. But he *had* been here before. He could sense it.

He wished Mimi were there so he could talk to her about it.

Inspector Cheddar rode up. 'This is the life!' he said. 'Adventure! Danger! The undiscovered world! I feel like a film star! And not a traffic cone in sight!'

'There's nothing glamorous about it,' Mrs Tucker scolded. 'It's very dangerous if you don't know what you're doing. It's lucky for you I'm here.'

Inspector Cheddar frowned. 'I'm in charge of this expedition, Mrs Tucker. Not you. I think you'll find I'm more than a match for Klob and those villains.'

'I'm not talking about Klob,' Mrs Tucker snorted. 'She's the least of our worries. I'm talking about the desert. You wouldn't last five minutes out here on your own.'

'Oh really!' Inspector Cheddar bridled. 'Wanna bet?'

134

Mrs Tucker raised her eyebrows. She was about to say something rude when her camel farted loudly.

Mr Tucker lumbered up. He sniffed. 'Blimey! That stuff's more powerful than shaarrrk faaarrrt. I's goin' to bottle it and take it home for me boat.' He rummaged around for an old water bottle in his pack.

'I'm thirsty,' Michael complained.

'Can we stop soon?' Callie asked.

'Yes, all right,' Mrs Tucker agreed. It was approaching noon and they had been on the go since before dawn. They wanted to get as far as possible before the sun was at its hottest. 'We'll make camp over there by those rocks and rest until the sun goes down.'

'I'll take it from here,' Inspector Cheddar said bossily, when they reached the rocks. He whipped out his notebook.

'What's that for?' Mrs Tucker asked.

'The Chief Inspector of Bigsworth asked me to file a report,' Inspector Cheddar told her.

Mrs Tucker snorted. 'Of you making a fool of yourself.'

'Thank you, Mrs Tucker.' Inspector Cheddar glared at her. 'You can stand down. I'll take it from here.'

'Darling, I don't think that's a good idea . . .' Mrs Cheddar began.

'Let him, if he thinks he can,' Mrs Tucker said. Her camel lurched forward on to its elbows, then collapsed its back legs. Atticus waited for Mrs Tucker to get off, and jumped into her basket. He couldn't walk on the sun-soaked sand. It gave him blisters on his paws. They waited in the shade with the rest of the group while Inspector Cheddar explored the rocks for the best place to shelter.

'I used to be a boy scout.' Inspector Cheddar's voice floated over the rocks. 'Don't worry. You're in safe hands.'

'Here.' Mrs Tucker poured Atticus some water into a bowl. The others drank thirstily from their bottles. 'Don't waste it,' Mrs Tucker cautioned. 'We need to make it last.'

'I've found somewhere!' Inspector Cheddar called. Making sure the camels were safely tethered out of the sun,

Mrs Tucker led the others through the rocks to join him. Atticus was still in the basket. 'This'll be good!' she muttered.

Inspector Cheddar was standing at the mouth of a cave scribbling in his notebook.

'See?' he said. 'I told you I could lead the expedition. I've found us a nice shady cave to shelter in.'

'Have you checked it?' Mrs Tucker said, picking Atticus out and setting him down on some cool sand.

'What for?' Inspector Cheddar asked.

'Scorpions, snakes, spiders,' Mrs Tucker reeled off a list. 'Bugs, bats, lizards, creepy-crawlies, beetles, mice, lice, flies, locusts, mites, centipedes, millipedes, trillipedes, zillipedes and sand fleas.' She pulled on a pair of gloves.

'Er . . .' Inspector Cheddar said.

SSSSSSSSSSSSSSSSSSSSSS.

'What was that?' Mrs Cheddar whispered.

SSSSSSSSSSSSSSSSSSSSSS.

The noise was coming from somewhere behind Inspector Cheddar. He gulped.

'*Freeze!*' Mrs Tucker hissed.

Inspector Cheddar froze.

SSSSSSSSSSSSSSSSSSSSSSSS.

A large snake started to uncoil from a pile of stones at the cave entrance. Atticus growled. The snake was greyish brown on the top and a wormy pink underneath. It was perfectly camouflaged against the dusty stones. It advanced towards Inspector Cheddar, raised its head slowly and puffed out its hood.

'It's a cobra!' Mr Tucker sucked his teeth. 'I don't rate your chances, matey. They's worse than eels for biting. Deadly, cobras is.' He shook his head sadly. 'But don't worry,' he added brightly, 'it'll be over so quick youze won't feel a thing.'

SSSSSSSSSSSSSSSSSSSSSSSS.

Callie started to cry. Mrs Cheddar went white. Michael trembled violently.

'You're not helping, Herman!' Mrs Tucker scolded. 'Unscrew your wooden leg.'

'But . . .'

'Just do it!' Mrs Tucker ordered.

Mr Tucker sat down slowly and started unscrewing his leg.

SSSSSSSSSSSSSSSSSS.

The cobra swayed towards Inspector Cheddar.

Atticus swallowed. He had a bad feeling about what was coming next.

'Atticus, I need your help,' Mrs Tucker whispered. 'You'll have to create a diversion. Get it away from the Inspector and I'll whack it with Mr Tucker's leg.'

I knew it! Atticus sighed heavily. He hated snakes. They made his fur prickle. All the cats he had ever known hated snakes, apart from Ginger Biscuit, who smacked them with his spiked collar before killing them to show off. But Atticus realised he had no choice. He had to help the Cheddars.

Atticus took a deep breath and eased his way along the cooler sand towards the entrance of the cave, skirting the rocks so that the snake didn't see him. He needed to make sure Mrs Tucker had a clean shot. He stopped. The snake was between him and Inspector Cheddar. Inspector Cheddar grinned at him weakly. The Inspector was sweating. His face was chalky white. He wouldn't be able to stay still much longer.

Atticus inched forward: it was hard to judge

how long the snake was when one end of it was still coiled up. He glanced at Mrs Tucker. She had the wooden leg in her hand poised to throw. There was nothing in her way. Atticus hoped she was a good aim!

'Rrrrrrrrrrrrrr,' he growled.

SSSSSSSSSSSSSSSSSSSSS.

The snake turned. Its cold eyes met his. It began to uncoil. Any minute now and it would strike.

With a fierce yowl, Atticus fluffed out his fur. Fear kicked in. His skin prickled. His fur stood on end, as if he'd had an electric shock. He puffed up to double his normal size.

For an instant the snake was startled. It drew back. Then it gathered itself to strike. Atticus closed his eyes. He waited for the venomous bite.

THWACK!

Atticus opened his eyes again.

The snake lay dead a few inches away from his forepaws. Mr Tucker's wooden leg rolled to and fro in the sand beside it.

Inspector Cheddar fainted. The children and Mrs Cheddar ran to him. Mrs Tucker strode over to collect Atticus. She chucked the wooden leg back to Mr Tucker.

'Thanks, Herman,' she said. She picked Atticus up and stroked him calmly until his fur began to subside. 'Phew!' she whispered. 'That was scary!'

Atticus meowed his agreement.

'And we haven't even got to Nebu-Mau yet!' She retrieved a mobile phone from her basket and dialled a number. 'Badawi?' she said. 'It's Agent Whelk. We could use your help.' She glanced at Atticus. 'And bring some of your best warriors.'

14

A few miles further into the desert, the magpies were having a rotten time. They were sharing a camel with Biscuit, who was hogging the saddle while the magpies clung on to the hump, except for Pig who was hanging on to the camel's tail. Mimi was up ahead with Professor Verry-Clever. Klob was at the front of the camel train. The Tofflys brought up the rear.

'I hate this place,' Slasher panted.

'It's like an oven,' Gizzard gasped.

'I'm being roasted alive,' Wally wheezed.

'I think this camel's been sitting in Zenia's poo-bucket.' Pig choked on the smell coming from the camel's bum.

'I need water!' Thug rattled. 'Water! Water!

I'm dying of thirst!'

'Yeah, and whose fault is that?' Ginger Biscuit looked at Thug murderously. He'd been in a worse mood than ever since they'd arrived in Egypt and found that the magpies had catnapped Mimi by mistake instead of Atticus. So had Zenia.

'I needed a bath!' Thug protested. 'I was all hot and sandy! My feathers get itchy if I don't shower regularly.'

'You didn't have to use the whole bottle!' Biscuit spat. 'That's our whole ration. Gone.'

'It's all right for you.' Jimmy eyed him with dislike. 'Zenia will give you some of her water. We're gonna have to beg the Professor again.'

'There's no food though, is there?' Biscuit was still glaring at Thug. 'Apart from lizards.'

'I was hungry!' Thug shrilled. 'I didn't realise that packet of dried stuff was meant to be for all of us. I thought it was just for me. If I don't eat regularly I get beak ache.'

'If we don't find this place soon,' Biscuit snarled, 'I'm going to pick you off one by one, starting with Thug, suck all your blood out and crunch the rest of you, bones and all.'

'I'll tell Anubis if you do,' Thug threatened. 'He'll get the curse of the cat pharaoh down on you like a ton of worms.'

'Halt!' Zenia cried from the front of the camel train.

The camels knelt. Everyone got down.

'Vell?' Klob demanded.

'It should be somewhere near here.' The Professor scratched his hat. He pulled Howard Toffly's book out of his pocket and studied it. He squinted at the sun through dark glasses. He inspected the nearby rock formations. He consulted his camelometer, which told him how many miles they'd travelled. Finally he got out a compass and checked it.

Mimi watched him carefully.

'The path to the golden city lies through sand and water,' he said, frowning at the book. 'The hieroglyphs are very clear. By my calculations, the city is approximately sixty miles due west of Giza. The compass bearing is correct. I tell you, it should be here. Look at the shape of the rock formations.'

They looked. Mimi gave a little exclamation. The rocks were in the

144

shape of a cat's head.

'Well, it's not here,' Lord Toffly said. 'Can you see a city, Antonia?'

'I'm afraid I can't, Roderick,' Lady Toffly brayed.

'You're not Verry-Clever at all, are you?' Lord Toffly said rudely to the Professor. 'You're Verry-Stupid.'

Mimi felt sorry for Professor Verry-Clever. He was a nice man and he'd been kind to her since their kidnap, feeding her part of his rations to keep her spirits up as well as giving some of his water to those ungrateful magpies. She wondered where Atticus was. Zenia thought he'd come after them with Mrs Tucker and the Inspector to rescue her and the Professor and find the treasure. For once, Mimi hoped that Zenia was right. She glanced back at the shifting dunes. The only good thing about being stuck in the desert was that it gave Atticus and Mrs Tucker more of a chance to find them. If they got to the golden city of cats before Atticus reached them, there was no telling what would happen.

'There's certainly plenty of sand,' Klob agreed. 'But not much vater.'

She turned to Biscuit. 'Vot should I do vith him, Biscuit? Vot about burying him up to his neck in the sand until he comes up vith something useful?'

'Good idea,' agreed Lord Toffly.

'Bravo!' said Lady Toffly.

Mimi gaped at Zenia in horror. *She wouldn't!* she whispered.

Biscuit sidled up to her. He grinned slyly. 'Yes, she would.'

'But he's doing his best!' Mimi meowed.

Biscuit ignored her. 'Still hoping your boyfriend's going to show up?' he said.

Mimi didn't answer.

'Well, I am.' Biscuit bared his sharp teeth. 'So that I can chew other bits of him besides his ear.' He popped out a set of claws. POP. POP. POP. POP. 'Once he's got us into the tomb, of course.'

'He won't get you into the tomb,' Mimi said.

'You reckon?' Biscuit rippled his shoulder muscles. 'I think he will, when he sees I mean to sacrifice *you* to Cattypuss the Great.'

'Chaka-chaka-chaka-chaka-chaka!'

The magpies hopped and chattered in a tired,

146

hot sort of way. That was the best news they'd heard all day.

'We'll help,' Jimmy squawked.

'Count me out.' Thug pulled a face. 'I don't like the sight of blood. I'll just come along after you've finished sacrificing and help myself to a bit of treasure if that's okay.'

Ginger put a hunky paw around Mimi's shoulder. He let out a puff of lizard-smelling breath. 'That is, unless you wanted to be the next queen of Nebu-Mau?' He suggested casually.

'What are you talking about?' Mimi shrugged him off. She pretended to wipe sand out of her whiskers. She didn't want Ginger Biscuit to see that she was afraid of him.

Biscuit examined his claws. 'Once Claw's out of the way I might become the next cat pharaoh. You could be my queen.'

'Oooohhhh!' Thug whistled. 'I think he likes you!'

'I'd rather be sacrificed,' Mimi said in disgust. 'And anyway, you could never be a cat pharaoh. You don't have what it takes.'

'Ooohhhhh!' Slasher hooted. 'Get her.'

'You'll regret that,' Ginger Biscuit snarled. 'And you might change your mind when you see what I've got in store for Claw.'

'Get the shovel!' Klob cried. 'Let's dig a hole for the Professor.'

'No!' Professor Verry-Clever pleaded. 'I promise you. The path to the lost city is here somewhere.'

''Ere, Slash,' Thug was staring into the distance. 'You see those rocks that look like a cat's head?'

'Yeah.'

'Well, go right a bit.'

'Yeah.'

'Where the valley is.'

'Yeah. What about it?'

'Can't you see it?'

'All I can see is sand, Thug mate.'

'Are you blind?' Thug blinked at the desert. 'It's right there.'

'What is?'

'The swimming pool.' Thug's eyes popped. 'It's next to the stripy deck chairs and the bar with cocktails lined up along the top. Derr.'

Wally shook his head. 'He's hal-loo-cinating,' he muttered. 'That's what happens in the desert.

His brain's been scrambled by the heat, like an egg.'

'Well, aren't you coming?' Thug summoned his remaining energy and flapped off. 'Last one in the pool's a pair of big girl's pants.'

'Vere is that magpie going?' Zenia shrieked. 'I vill not have mutiny amongst my slaves. After him, Biscuit.'

Biscuit chased across the sand after Thug.

Mimi watched him go. Even in this heat Biscuit still had the stamina to run. And the blistering sand didn't seem to hurt his paws. Atticus would have to use all his intelligence to defeat him. *If he came.* Mimi stifled a sniff. Professor Verry-Clever seemed to sense there was something wrong. He put out a bony hand to stroke her. She nuzzled him affectionately to show him he did at least have one friend.

Thug had made it past the rocks into the valley. The imaginary swimming pool sparkled before him in the sun, blue and cool and inviting. He put his wings forward and dived.

CRUNCH!

Thug landed beak down in the sand. He sat up, bewildered. 'Where'd it go?' he demanded.

Biscuit advanced on him. 'Bye, bye, barmy birdie!' he said. POP. POP. POP. POP.

CRACK!

Biscuit stopped. 'What's happening?'

CRACK! CRACK! CRACK! CRACK!

The ground shuddered.

WHOOSH!

Suddenly water burst through the earth and gushed upwards in huge fountains.

'My shower!' Thug rejoiced, fluffing his feathers out to feel the drops.

Biscuit grabbed him in his teeth and retreated to the safety of the rocks.

'That's it!' Professor Verry-Clever gathered Mimi in his arms and stumbled towards them.

Klob and the Tofflys followed with the camels.

'That's the path!' the Professor yelled. 'Through sand and water! I told you. The bird must have triggered some kind of minor earthquake.'

'Nice one, Thug!' Gizzard gave him a pat.

'What d'I do?' Thug looked round, puzzled.

The fountains became a lake. Soon the valley was flooded.

'But where's the lost city?' Lord Toffly puffed.

At that moment the water parted. It formed two towering columns either side of a deep jagged crack in the valley floor where the water had burst through.

'Down there.' Professor Verry-Clever pointed.

The beginnings of a golden staircase glittered tantalisingly between the sheets of water before disappearing down into the crevasse.

'Chaka-chaka-chaka-chaka-chaka!' The magpies chattered excitedly.

'It's real!' Jimmy's eyes gleamed. 'Let's go get the treasure, boys.' He spread his wings. 'And then we'll get Claw.'

'MMYYYAAAWWWW!' Biscuit let out a savage howl. He pinned Jimmy by the tail. 'The treasure's mine and Zenia's, beakface. Don't you forget it. You get what we don't want. That's all.' He flattened his ears. His voice dropped to a hiss. 'And *I get Claw.*'

'Chaka-chaka-chaka-chaka-chaka!'

'Take vot you need from the camels,' Zenia instructed the humans. 'Then ve'll proceed.' She glanced back in the direction they had come. 'Atticus and Velk von't be far behind. And ven they come, I, Zenia Klob, mistress of disguise, and my evil cat Biscuit, vill be vaiting for them. Ah ha ha ha ha ha! Ah ha ha ha!' She marched off back to the camels to get her suitcase of Egyptian dressing-up costumes.

Mimi watched her go. The wind was getting up. Sand was starting to fly everywhere. They would have to hurry or they would get caught in a sandstorm. *The path to the lost city lies through sand and water.* If they made it through the lake, the staircase should take them to Nebu-Mau and to the tomb of the cat pharaoh. But would Atticus be able to follow? Her golden eyes fixed on the horizon. 'Atticus,' she whispered desperately. 'Where are you? Please hurry!'

Badawi and his group of Bedouin warriors joined Atticus and his friends at the cave. They brought with them some racing camels, which were a lot faster than the ones Mrs Tucker had hired. Badawi sent the other ones back to his tribe with one of the warriors. Everyone was glad to see them go, except Mr Tucker who had become quite fond of his. He'd managed to collect several bottles of camel fart.

'I'll name me next boat in your honour,' he shouted after the camel. 'I promise.'

As soon as it became cooler, they set off at a brisk canter across the desert in the direction they thought Klob and the villains had taken. It was late evening when they reached the cat's-head rocks.

The sun was setting. They dismounted from the camels and tethered them in the shade.

'We must be close to the lost city,' Mrs Tucker said, eyeing the rocks.

Badawi bent down to examine the sand for tracks.

'Have they been here?' Mrs Cheddar asked.

'It's hard to say,' Badawi replied. 'There's been a sandstorm.' He looked at the sky nervously. 'We should probably go. We don't want to get caught in it if there's another one.'

Atticus felt anxious. What if Mimi had been hurt in the sandstorm? Or lost? But he didn't want to go. This was the place. Nebu-Mau was very near.

'Get a whiff of that!' Mr Tucker had found some camel dung. He stuck his nose close and breathed deeply. 'Aaaaahhhh, lovely.'

'So they *were* here!' Mrs Tucker exclaimed.

'Not long ago. It's still fresh.' Badawi examined it. 'Only a few hours old.'

'Where could they have gone?' Michael asked.

'Maybe they found the path to the lost city,' Mrs Cheddar said, pointing to the lake. 'The hieroglyphs said it lies through sand and water.'

Badawi and the warriors stared at the flooded valley. They spoke to one another in hushed whispers.

'What's the matter?' Mrs Tucker said sharply.

'Last time we were here, that lake wasn't,' Badawi told her.

'Are you sure?'

Badawi consulted his warriors. 'They all agree. Last time it was desert. Now it's an oasis. There hasn't been water here for thousands of years. Since the time of Cattypuss the Great.'

'You know about Cattypuss?' Mrs Cheddar asked.

Badawi nodded. 'It is a legend amongst my people. There were rumours the stranger summoned the water a century ago, but no one saw it.'

'The stranger? You mean Howard Toffly?' Mrs Tucker guessed.

Badawi nodded. 'My people told him of the curse, but he wouldn't listen. He wanted to find the lost city. One day he disappeared. He was mad by the time he returned to the Bedouin.'

'We think he did summon the water,' Mrs Tucker said grimly. 'We think he found the city. We think he stole a book from the cat pharaoh's tomb. That's why he was cursed.'

Badawi shuddered. He said something to his men. They looked uneasy. 'They do not wish to go any further,' he said. 'They are afraid.'

'Tell them they are safe,' Mrs Tucker said.

'How?'

'Because Atticus is a descendant of Cattypuss the Great,' she explained. 'The cat pharaoh won't harm us while he's around.'

Atticus was studying the landscape. It all seemed so familiar. It was like coming home. A gentle wind rippled his fur. The desert was cooling rapidly as the night drew in. It didn't feel hostile any more. And something told him Mimi wasn't far away. She had gone to the lost city. She was safe, for now. He felt his paws turn in the direction of the rock formation. Before he knew what was happening he had leapt on to it and scrambled to the top. He sat between the cat's ears facing the flooded valley, raised a paw in the direction of the lake and let out a brief meow.

'Would you look at that!' Mrs Tucker breathed.

All at once the lake began to part. It separated into two towering walls of water. Between them, in a deep crevasse, shimmered the beginnings of a golden staircase.

Badawi and his men looked on in disbelief.

'Atticus!' Michael had been watching him.

'He did that!' Callie let out a breath.

'He really is an amazing cat!' Mrs Cheddar's voice was hushed.

Even Inspector Cheddar was impressed. He got out his notebook at once. 'I must tell the Chief Inspector of Bigsworth about this,' he said.

At that moment the wind got up. It whipped through the sand. Within seconds they were enveloped in a thick cloud of choking dust.

'Quick!' yelled Badawi. 'It's a sandstorm. We have to find cover.'

Mrs Cheddar grabbed the children.

'Where's Atticus?' cried Michael.

The wind howled.

'He's here!' Callie reached down. Atticus had climbed down from the rocks and was nudging at her ankles. 'He wants us to follow him.'

'Get in a line!' Mrs Tucker ordered.

They did as they were told.

'Hang on to this.' Badawi passed a rope along the line of frightened humans and showed them how to loop it around their waists. 'Everyone stay together.'

'What about the camels?' Michael cried.

'They'll be fine,' Badawi said. 'They'll find shelter. My people will come for them when the storm is finished.'

'It's like the time I got caught in Hurricane Haddock!' Mr Tucker boomed. 'Only it's raining sand, not haddock.'

Atticus was at the head of the line. He allowed Mrs Tucker to pass the rope through the handkerchief around his neck. 'Go on, then, Atticus,' she said. 'Show us where to go.'

Atticus led them towards the lake. The sand made it difficult to see where he was going, but his instinct led him on.

'My notebook!' From somewhere near the back Inspector Cheddar let out a cry of anguish. 'It's blown away.' He untied himself.

Badawi tried to grab him but Inspector Cheddar

158

had already disappeared in the blizzard of sand.

'Don't worry!' Badawi shouted. 'I'll find him. We'll catch you up!'

The others struggled forward. Eventually they reached the edge of the lake. They started along the tunnel through the water. The wind blew even harder. The sand whipped at their faces and clothes. The water churned either side of them. If it came down on top of them they'd be smashed to pieces.

'The path through sand and water,' Mrs Tucker shouted. 'I wasn't expecting it to be both at the same time!'

They battled towards the golden staircase. Every step was an effort. Only Atticus seemed unfazed by the wind and the towering water. He barely flinched, padding slowly and patiently so they could keep up with him.

Eventually they reached their goal. Atticus stepped on to the golden staircase. The children scrambled after him with Mrs Cheddar, who quickly untied the rope from around his neck. Mrs Tucker was next. Then Mr Tucker.

'Phew!' Mrs Tucker said. 'That's better.'

The wind had become still. The blowing sand

had disappeared. It was as if they had reached another world.

Atticus stood on the top step looking down.

There was a hullabaloo behind them. One of the Bedouin warriors was shouting something in Arabic. The others joined in. They tumbled on to the golden steps, shouting and pointing.

Michael looked back. His eyes widened in horror. 'The water's closing in!' he screamed.

Inspector Cheddar and Badawi were making their way against the sandstorm through the tunnel of water. Behind them the great columns descended, crashing and churning like an avalanche.

'They're not going to make it!' Callie shrieked.

Atticus turned. As soon as he saw what was happening, he dodged past the humans and sprinted back through the tunnel of water towards the struggling men.

'Atticus!' Mrs Cheddar screeched.

Then something amazing happened. The water behind the two men stopped crashing and churning. Instead it began to re-form into columns. The further Atticus went down the tunnel, the further the water receded. By the time he reached Inspector Cheddar and Badawi, the tunnel was safe.

Atticus guided them to the golden staircase where the others were waiting.

'Darling!' Mrs Cheddar hugged Inspector Cheddar.

'Badawi!' Mrs Tucker hugged Badawi.

'Warriooorrrs!' Mr Tucker and the Bedouin warriors hugged one another.

Michael and Callie wanted to hug Atticus, but they both hesitated to pick him up. There was something different about Atticus: something mysterious and powerful.

'Only the true descendant of Cattypuss the Great has the power to hold back the water,' Badawi whispered. He knelt in front of Atticus. 'I thank you.'

'Er, so do I,' Inspector Cheddar said rather uncomfortably. 'Although I wish I'd found my notebook.' He coughed.

Atticus purred faintly. He was glad he'd been able to save Inspector Cheddar and Badawi, but he felt embarrassed by all the attention. He didn't like what was happening to him. He didn't want to have special powers. All Atticus wanted was to be back at number 2 Blossom Crescent with the Cheddars and Mimi, eating sardines and lying in his basket. He wanted to get back to police-catting. He wanted to go to Nellie Smellie's and make sure the abandoned kittens were staying out of trouble. Being the true descendant of Cattypuss the Great wasn't his scene, especially as everyone treated him differently as a result. He didn't want Badawi to kneel before him (although it would still be nice if Inspector Cheddar could do a bit of worshipping). His ears drooped. He wanted a tickle. But no one, not even Callie and Michael, seemed to want to touch him. Instead, everyone just stared. He looked at the floor.

'Poor Atticus!'

'He looks miserable!'

'Do you think he's missing Mimi?'

To his delight he felt someone scoop him up. It was Michael.

'You're still our cat, aren't you, Atticus?' Michael asked him anxiously.

Atticus purred throatily.

'Of course he is.' Callie gave him a kiss on the nose.

Atticus wriggled a bit so that she could tickle his tummy. His legs dangled in the air. He was beginning to feel a bit better.

'He'd never leave us,' Mrs Cheddar said, holding his paw. 'Would you, Atticus?'

''Course he wouldn't.' Mr Tucker patted his head.

Mrs Tucker was looking at Atticus thoughtfully. 'He'd never leave us,' she said, 'but that doesn't mean we might not lose him if we're not careful. He may be in great danger.'

'From Klob and Biscuit you mean?' Michael said.

'No,' Mrs Tucker said solemnly. 'From Cattypuss the Great.'

16

They began to descend the golden staircase.

The strange thing about it was that although their feet seemed to be taking them down into the earth, their brains told them that they weren't really going down at all. Instead of getting darker, the further along the staircase they travelled, the *lighter* it became.

Atticus led the way. The light drew him on. That and knowing that he would soon see Mimi. And something else: a feeling he couldn't name. Mimi called it instinct. So did Mrs Tucker. But this was more than instinct: it was more than just knowing or remembering things. It was as if something or someone had *control* of him. It was the same feeling he'd had at Howard Toffly's crypt the first time he went, when he couldn't move his paws. It was the same force that had driven him back to the crypt in a trance to rescue the ancient book before the magpies got hold of it. It was the same power that had sent him to the top of the cat's-head rock formation to lift his paw and reveal the path through sand and water.

Even if Mimi and the Professor hadn't been in danger, even if he'd wanted to stop and go back, he knew couldn't. The force was overwhelming. It was taking possession of him.

He padded on. The others followed. On either side of them shimmered a soft golden haze. It was like fog, Atticus thought, except it wasn't cold or damp. Gradually the haze began to clear. He looked down at his paws. They were standing on a huge golden barge in the middle of the flooded valley. The staircase had disappeared.

He glanced behind. There was no sign of the towering columns of water. There was barely a whisper of wind. And around the lake wasn't desert, but green palm trees as far as he could see. Behind him on the hill, the same cat's-head rocks stared down at them. Ahead of him,

165

glowing in the sun, was the golden city of cats.

'Nebu-Mau!' Mrs Tucker said. 'We've arrived.'

'A baaarrrrge!' Mr Tucker hopped about in glee, making the barge roll from side to side. 'At laaarrrst!'

'Stop it, Herman, you're making us feel sick,' Mrs Tucker complained.

Mr Tucker broke into a sea shanty. He was thrilled to be back on a boat.

'The laaarrrst time I was on a lake,
I caught meself a giant hake,
It wriggled and it thrashed when I hooked it,
So I bashed it with me wooden leg and cooked it.'

Mrs Tucker glared at him. 'Very interesting, Herman, I'm sure. Now can we go?'

'Grab an oaaarrr,' Mr Tucker commanded. 'Apart from youze, Atticus. Youze can help me navigate.'

Atticus hopped on to the tiller. The others took the oars.

'Heave!' Mr Tucker gave the order.

They heaved.

166

The barge edged forward.

'I said "Heave"!' Mr Tucker shouted.

'Why don't *you* heave?' Mrs Tucker muttered.

'Because I's the captain,' Mr Tucker bellowed. 'I's in charge of this vessel. Now HEAVE or I'll have to make you walk the plank!'

Soon the barge was skimming through the water.

'I name this baarrrge *The Crafty Camel*,' Mr Tucker said.

Atticus gazed straight ahead. The breeze tickled his whiskers. The sensation was familiar. He'd been here before.

He remembered the flooded valley and the palm trees and the golden haze on the water. He recalled the barge and the cat's-head rocks. And more than anything, he remembered Nebu-Mau: the golden city of cats. *His* city. *His* home. *His* people.

Atticus shook his head. *What was he thinking?* This wasn't his home! Blossom Crescent was. He lived in Littleton-on-Sea, England, not in Nebu-Mau, Western Desert, Egypt. The Cheddars were his people.

He swallowed. It was as if he was getting his

wires crossed between two different lives.

They were approaching the harbour.

'Drop the oars!' Mr Tucker steered the barge expertly alongside the wooden dock. He jumped out and tied the barge. The others clambered out. Atticus hopped on to the dock. A second barge was moored a few metres away but there was no sign of anyone on board. He looked along the shoreline. There was no one else around. Nebu-Mau seemed completely deserted.

'Klob's got to be here somewhere,' Mrs Tucker said. 'Atticus, where's the tomb?'

Atticus lifted his head. They followed his gaze.

Before them a wide boulevard led through the city from the harbour. On either side of it were rows of magnificent buildings decorated in hieroglyphs. They were like the ones Atticus had seen in Howard Toffly's crypt. And everywhere you looked there were statues of the cat pharaoh, painted in brown and black stripes, with four white paws and large green eyes. They were statues of *him* except instead of a red handkerchief he was wearing a blue and green headdress.

'Atticus!' Callie whispered.

'No,' said Mrs Tucker quickly. 'It's not Atticus. It's Cattypuss the Great.'

'But . . .' Michael started.

'They're not the same, Michael.' Mrs Tucker's expression was deadly serious. 'It's really important you remember that.'

At the end of the boulevard was a pyramid. Even from this distance they could see it was encased in gold.

'That's where Klob will be,' Mrs Tucker said. 'She knows Atticus will come after Mimi. She'll be holding her prisoner somewhere in the pyramid. You can bet your barnacles. She'll be lying in wait for us.'

'So what's the plan?' Badawi asked.

'We've going to let her capture us,' Mrs Tucker said.

'What?' Michael shouted.

'But what about Atticus?' Callie cried.

'Biscuit will kill him as soon as he shows them how to get into Cattypuss's tomb!' Mrs Cheddar protested.

'What Klob doesn't know,' Mrs Tucker explained patiently, 'is that Badawi's here with the warriors. If she thinks she's captured all of us, she'll be off her guard. That's when Badawi and his men strike.'

'It's too dangerous,' Mrs Cheddar said immediately.

Atticus held out his paw. He wanted to let her know that he would do it. He wasn't afraid of Biscuit. Something told him he could handle him. Or at least that Cattypuss could.

'Are you sure, Atticus?' Michael said.

Atticus purred.

Callie hugged him.

'Now don't get all sentimental,' Mrs Tucker said briskly. 'When I said we'd let Klob capture us, I didn't say we'd *stay* captured, did I?'

The children smiled.

'Don't youze worry.' Mr Tucker was chewing his pipe thoughtfully. 'I'll make sure those villains rue the day they messed with me beard-jumper.'

Badawi nodded. 'We'll hide out nearby. We'll be ready. And if Atticus does open the tomb, we'll make sure it's the Egyptian government that gets the treasure for the nation, not Klob and the Tofflys.'

'And then Dad can arrest them. Can't you, Dad?' Callie said.

There was no reply.

'Dad?' Michael looked around.

'Where's he gone?' Mrs Cheddar said, puzzled.

'I's dunno. He was here a minute ago,' Mr Tucker said.

'For halibut's sake!' Mrs Tucker exclaimed. 'I wish he'd stop disappearing like this.'

'Maybe he went to see if he could find another notebook,' Callie suggested. 'He seems really worried about filing his report for the Chief Inspector of Bigsworth.'

'He's a stickler for procedure,' Mrs Cheddar sighed.

'Well, he's not going to find a notebook here, is he?' said Mrs Tucker, exasperated. 'We'll have to find him later. Ready, Badawi?'

Badawi nodded. 'We'll meet you at the pyramid.'

Inspector Cheddar was disappointed. Sure, Nebu-Mau was filled with priceless treasure and about a billion statues of a cat that looked a lot like Atticus, but it was very low on notebook shops. In fact, as

171

far as he could tell there was nowhere in this darned place that he could so much as borrow a scrap of paper from. There were no newsagents, no corner shops, no stationers and no book shops. There were no offices or banks or libraries or police stations. Just a lot of empty buildings with funny pictures carved on the walls.

Inspector Cheddar was just wondering how he was going to explain to the Chief Inspector of Bigsworth why he hadn't kept a log of the investigation when he heard a noise.

Squeak . . . squeak . . . squeak.

He listened hard.

Squeak . . . squeak . . . squeak.

A man in a white djellaba and a turban appeared from around a corner. He was pushing a small cart full of melons. 'Need help?' he asked.

Inspector Cheddar nodded. 'Can you please tell me where I can buy a notebook? It's very urgent.'

'Vill papyrus do?' The man offloaded a few melons. At the bottom of the cart was a box full of papyrus scrolls.

'I'll have the lot!' Inspector Cheddar grabbed the box. 'You got any biros?'

'Qvill pens only,' the man said.

'I'll take ten,' Inspector Cheddar said.

The man counted out ten quill pens and handed them to the Inspector. 'That vill be vun thousand Egyptian pounds.'

'What? That's daylight robbery!' Inspector Cheddar complained. He got ready to haggle. 'I'll give you fifty pence.'

'Forget it.'

'Okay, a pound.'

'Nope.'

Inspector Cheddar emptied his pockets. He only had a bit of change. He hadn't brought much money with him: there wasn't much to buy in the desert.

The man was watching him closely. 'Don't vaste my time,' he said nastily. 'Give me back my papyrus and my qvill pens.'

'No. You don't understand. I'm a policeman,' Inspector Cheddar admitted in desperation. 'I have to file a report to the Chief Inspector of Bigsworth.'

The papyrus seller looked interested. 'Really? Vot about?'

Inspector Cheddar looked around to make sure they weren't being overheard. 'I'm on the trail of a vicious criminal. Her name's Klob. She's a mistress of disguise. You haven't seen her, have you?' he asked hopefully.

The papyrus seller shook his head. 'I don't think so,' he said. 'Vot does she look like?'

Inspector Cheddar pulled a horrible face. 'She's an ugly bruiser.'

The papyrus seller frowned. 'Ugly?'

'Hideous.' Inspector Cheddar nodded. 'She's got a face like a camel's bum.'

The papyrus seller went red. 'How dare you insult a lady like that!' he shouted.

'She's not a lady, she's a disgusting old hag,' Inspector Cheddar protested. 'Trust me. I'd rather kiss a warthog.'

The papyrus seller frothed at the mouth. He reached under his turban. 'You've done it now!' He produced a fistful of sharp-looking pins.

Inspector Cheddar realised his mistake. 'Miss Klob!' he gasped. 'I didn't mean it. You've got a face to sink a thousand ships.'

'The saying is *launch* a thousand ships, not *sink* them, you vally. And it's Ms, not Miss,' Zenia Klob shouted.

ZIP!

The first hairpin struck Inspector Cheddar in the neck. He folded to the ground.

'Vun dose of sleeping potion is not enough for you!' Zenia Klob screeched.

ZIP! ZIP! ZIP! ZIP! ZIP!

The other hairpins struck him in the chest, the leg, the arm, and one in each bum cheek.

Zenia Klob shook her fist at Inspector Cheddar's sleeping form. 'Ven you vake up – IF you vake up – you von't have a clue who you are.' She gave him a kick with the steel toe of her boot. 'Biscuit!'

Ginger Biscuit appeared from behind a building.

'Put him somewhere no one vill find him. A dungeon if possible. Full of spiders.'

'RRRRRRRR.' Ginger Biscuit took hold of Inspector Cheddar's foot with his front paws and dragged him into one of the buildings. After a few minutes he re-emerged covered in cobwebs.

'Good boy.' Zenia Klob gave him a beetle to chew. 'That vos a piece of luck getting Cheddar out of the vay. Now ve can go back to the pyramid and lie in vait for Atticus and the rest of his pals.'

17

Ginger Biscuit slouched back to the pyramid feeling murderous. Chewing a beetle didn't make his temper any better. Despite the lure of treasure, despite the pyramid of gold, despite even the fact that Zenia had promised him he could kill the magpies and roast them for dinner, he HATED the lost city of Nebu-Mau. He DESPISED the golden city of cats. It wasn't the golden city of *cats* anyway. That was the prob-

lem. It was the golden city of CAT. And that cat wasn't him. It was Cattypuss the Great.

Except that Cattypuss the Great looked like Atticus. Everybody said so: Professor

Verry-Clever, Mimi, the Tofflys, the magpies, even Zenia! Professor Verry-Clever was the worst. He kept getting the names mixed up: Atticus/Cattypuss, Atticus/Cattypuss, Atticus/Cattypuss. In fact Professor Verry-Clever had got himself so mixed up he'd started talking about *Atticus* the Great when they entered the pyramid.

Biscuit couldn't stand it. He couldn't stomach the idea that Atticus was the descendant of a cat pharaoh. He couldn't bear having to hang around until Atticus opened Cattypuss's tomb. It wasn't fair. Atticus was a coward. He was a police cat, a traitor, a piece of cat scum. The idea that Atticus was superior to him made Ginger Biscuit want to puke.

Ginger Biscuit wasn't just jealous. He was madly, vilely, bitterly, excruciatingly, *insanely* jealous. HE wanted to be a cat pharaoh. HE wanted to have a tomb full of treasure. HE wanted to have a boulevard of statues built in his honour. HE wanted his picture drawn on the wall of every building. He wanted people to bring HIM gifts. He dreamed of Professor Verry-Clever waiting on him with plates piled high with rats. He imagined sitting on a jewel-encrusted throne while the Tofflys plucked the magpies for him to nibble. He longed for Zenia to shower him with pike heads from her wheelie trolley. But what had he got instead? One measly beetle to crunch and fur full of cobwebs.

He stopped to wee on one of the two gigantic statues of Cattypuss the Great that guarded the pyramid, then slouched up the steps to the entrance behind Zenia into the first gloomy chamber.

'Go and make sure Atticus's girlfriend is tied up tight,' Zenia ordered him. 'And get those mangy magpies ready. I vant aerial bombardment as soon as Atticus opens the tomb. Lots of bird poo. Nice and smelly. The main target is Agent Velk and that stupid husband of hers. The Tofflys can deal with Mrs Cheesy and her repulsive kids. Go now, Biscuit. I'll get the Professor.'

Biscuit cast her an angry look.

'And don't be so grumpy, my little tomb-trashing tomcat!' Zenia added. 'You'll get vot you vant ven it's over. I'll even make you a cat pharaoh disguise if you like, out of the spare jewels.'

'Mmmyyyaaawww.' Biscuit didn't want a cat pharaoh *disguise*. He wanted to BE a cat pharaoh. Just at that moment nothing less would do.

He sloped off into the pyramid. He and Zenia had already cased the joint with the magpies. Professor Verry-Clever had shown them the way to the tomb, lighting torches as they went so that they wouldn't get lost. The tomb lay at the pyramid's heart: right under the pointy bit – so that Cattypuss could have a straight path to eternal life, according to the Professor. Well, stuff Cattypuss and his eternal life! It was Biscuit's turn to have a piece of the action. He eased his way along a labyrinth of passageways following the wall torches until he reached the antechamber to the tomb.

Mimi was tethered by the neck to an iron stake on an altar opposite the door.

'Comfortable?' Biscuit snarled.

'Perfectly, thank you.' Mimi turned her back on him and folded her front paws.

'Inspector Cheddar's not going to help you,' Biscuit told her. 'He's away with the pharaohs. Zenia hairpinned him. Six times. He'll sleep till Christmas.'

'Good for her,' Mimi said coldly.

Biscuit growled. Nothing he did or said seemed to make any impression on her.

'You can't escape, you know.'

'Yes I can,' Mimi said. 'Atticus will get me out.'

'MMMYYYAAAWWW!'

'And even if he doesn't, you're finished.'

'What do you mean?' Biscuit spat back.

'Cattypuss the Great's not going to be very pleased, is he, when he finds out you've killed one of his descendants,' Mimi said. 'He'll curse you, just like he did Howard Toffly. I wouldn't be surprised if he didn't hunt you down and throttle you. You'll be dead in your basket before you can say "obelisk".'

Biscuit's eyes narrowed.

'You hadn't thought of that, had you?' Mimi sensed she'd scored a victory. 'I wouldn't like to be in your paws when the curse of Cattypuss comes knocking.'

'GGRRRRRRR . . .'

The argument had woken up the magpies. They'd been having a sleep on a rush mat in the corner.

'Someone's in a bad mood!' sang Thug. He winked at Slasher. 'How many statues of Cattypuss the Great did you count on your way up the boulevard, Slash?'

'I got to one thousand, four hundred and eighty-nine,' Slasher said. 'Then I lost count: there were so many.'

'We'd better do it again on the way back.' Thug grinned. 'Will you help us, Ginger?'

'Cut it out!' Ginger Biscuit snapped.

'There's three thousand, one hundred and seven drawings of him in the passageway,' Pig said helpfully.

'Not to mention the etching on the altar,' Wally reminded them.

'And that lovely mural on the wall,' said Gizzard pointing at a large painting of Cattypuss the Great receiving gifts from minions.

'Shut up!' said Ginger Biscuit.

'It's amazing how much like Claw Cattypuss looks,' Slasher remarked.

'Could be his double!' Thug agreed. 'It's like Claw's really the cat pharaoh, not Cattypuss.'

There was a flash of ginger.

'Aaaaahhhhh!' shrieked Thug. 'He's pinned me tail!'

'Aaaaahhhhh!' screamed Slasher. 'He's got me bad foot!'

Ginger Biscuit dragged them to the altar. He took hold of another iron chain and tethered them both by the beak next to Mimi.

'Let them go,' Jimmy screeched.

'No.' Biscuit advanced on Pig, Wally and Gizzard. 'I've had it with you lot.' He pinned them too.

Pig and Gizzard fainted.

Wally pooed himself.

'Leave my magpies alone!' Jimmy hopped about in fury.

'Shan't.' Biscuit tethered the other three birds. He didn't care if Zenia was cross. He didn't care about anything except shutting the magpies up. And the curse: he cared about that.

'You can't do this!' Jimmy squawked. 'I forbid it!'

'Just watch me.' Ginger Biscuit grabbed Jimmy by the tail and slung him on the altar next to the others.

'Chaka-chaka-chaka-chaka-chaka!'

'Chaka-chaka-chaka-chaka-chaka!

'You've no right to sacrifice us!' Jimmy shouted, as Biscuit tied him up.

'Call it my little gift to Cattypuss,' Ginger Biscuit said. 'A little *offering* to take his mind off the main event. I'm sure he won't curse me when he sees what a lovely gift I've brought him. He's a cat, after all. He's bound to like birds.' Biscuit grinned at Mimi. 'Thanks for the tip.'

She backed away from the magpies. 'You beast,' she said.

'Squeamish, are you?' Ginger Biscuit popped out his claws. POP. POP. POP. POP. 'Wait till you see what I do to your boyfriend.'

The magpies squawked feebly.

Mimi looked away.

Just then the door to the antechamber was thrown open. Zenia burst in with Professor Verry-Clever and the Tofflys. Professor Verry-Clever had his hands tied behind his back. Zenia gave him a shove. He fell over and crawled into a corner.

'They're coming!' she shrieked. 'Atticus, Velk and the others. Positions, everyone!'

183

The villains dashed back into the labyrinth of passages to hide.

Ginger ran after them. 'I'll be back,' he hissed.

His time was coming. *Gingerpuss the Horrible.* He could almost hear the crowd roaring his name.

18

Inspector Cheddar opened one eye. He looked about. He was in a dingy cellar full of cobwebs. He opened the other eye and tried to sit up. 'Ouch!' He retrieved two hairpins from his backside and tried again.

Where was he? More to the point, *Who was he? What time was it? What YEAR WAS IT??* Inspector Cheddar couldn't remember a thing. He glanced at his clothes: a djellaba, a turban, some sandals. He felt in his pockets. A few quill pens and a bit of papyrus. He was an Ancient Egyptian. *But what did he do? What was his name?* A crack of light was coming from under the door. Inspector Cheddar pushed it open with a creak and started looking round for clues.

His eye was drawn to the hieroglyphs on the wall. There was a cat, a handsome, wise-looking tabby cat with four white socks and a blue and green headdress. Inspector Cheddar thought he'd seen that cat before. He traced the hieroglyphs with his fingers. Yes, it was all coming back to him now. The cat was the mighty ruler of Nebu-Mau: the cat pharaoh, Cattypuss the Great. Other hieroglyphs showed people coming from far and wide to worship him, bringing gifts and kneeling at his feet. Inspector Cheddar gave a cry of joy. *That was it!* He had come from afar to worship Cattypuss the Great: to offer himself up as his slave. He wished he had some prawns with him. He let himself out of the dungeon and trotted off towards the pyramid.

🐾

Atticus entered the pyramid with the Tuckers, the kids and Mrs Cheddar.

They made their way through the torch-lit passageways. Atticus felt calm. He knew the way. The others followed in silence. They entered the antechamber.

'Atticus!' Mimi cried. 'I knew you'd come!'

'Chaka-chaka-chaka-chaka-chaka!' Even the magpies were glad to see him!

'Mimi!' Atticus ran to her while Mrs Tucker went to rescue Professor Verry-Clever. Atticus flicked out his claws. It only took seconds for the world's greatest ex-cat burglar to free Mimi from the iron chain.

'Don't forget your old friends!' Thug pleaded.

'Let us out too!' Slasher begged.

Atticus hesitated. He didn't trust the magpies, but he didn't really want Biscuit to munch them either. They should face justice like any other criminal. He wondered where Inspector Cheddar was. He hoped he would come soon and arrest everyone. 'Maybe later,' he growled.

He turned to face the tomb. Mrs Tucker had untied Professor Verry-Clever. The Professor stood beside Atticus, Howard Toffly's book in his hand. His face was white. 'This is history in the making!' he whispered, giving Atticus a pat. 'Good luck, Atticus.'

'Are you sure you want to go through with this, Atticus?' Mrs Tucker asked.

Squeak . . . squeak . . . squeak.

They turned.

'Of course he's sure, Velk!' Zenia Klob marched into the antechamber. She had on her 1920s tomb-raider's costume: green khaki hat, green khaki jacket, green khaki shorts, green khaki knickers (although luckily you couldn't see those) and a pistol loaded with hairpins at her belt. 'Don't think I von't use it.' She took it out and waved it at Mrs Tucker.

The Tofflys stood behind her threateningly. Lord Toffly was very red in the face. His moustache shone with sweat. He had put his thickest tweed suit on for the occasion and it was very hot and itchy. He was armed with a set of dessertspoons. Lady Toffly had polished her teeth with Spoonbright. They shone yellow in the torchlight. She wore a T-shirt that said 'Tofflys' Treasure Trip', which she'd had printed specially in Cairo, and carried a sack to put the goodies in.

Biscuit pushed past them into the antechamber.

'Claw,' he hissed.

'Biscuit,' Atticus hissed back.

'Ve seem to be missing someone.' Klob

pretended to look for Inspector Cheddar. 'Ah yes, Inspector Vally.'

'Don't call Dad a wally,' Michael said.

'Vy not?' Klob spat. 'He said I had a face like a camel's bum.'

'You do have a face like a camel's bum!' Michael shouted back.

'Only a camel's bum is better looking!' Callie put her hands on her hips and stuck her tongue out at Zenia.

'Silence!' screeched Zenia. 'Dad's kaput. He von't save you. I vacked him vith six hairpins for his insolence.'

'No!' Mrs Cheddar screamed. 'You witch!'

'Shall ve proceed?' Zenia said coldly.

'MMMYAAAWWWW!' Biscuit howled his agreement.

Mimi touched Atticus's paw. Her golden eyes were anxious. 'Biscuit plans to kill you,' she whispered, 'as soon as you've entered the tomb.'

'It's okay, Mimi,' Atticus said. 'I think I know a way to defeat Biscuit.'

'How?'

'All these feelings I've been having,' Atticus

explained, 'they're partly instinct like you said. But I think it's more than that. I think Cattypuss is trying to control me. He *wants* me to open his tomb.'

'But why?' Mimi looked bewildered.

'Because he wants to come back to life. Cattypuss wants to be *me*. Or rather, he wants me to be *him*!'

Mimi looked horrified. 'But you're not him. He's not you. Atticus, you mustn't let him control you.'

'I have to, Mimi, just for a little while,' Atticus said. 'It's the only way.'

'No!' Mimi clutched his paw. 'It's too dangerous. What if he doesn't let you go? What if you never come back?'

Atticus set her paw down gently. 'I've thought of that,' he said, 'but I have to take the risk. To save my family. And the Professor. And you.'

He stepped forward.

The door to the tomb was covered in hieroglyphs. The symbols were different from the ones in Howard Toffly's book. They showed a funeral: a sarcophagus in the shape of the cat pharaoh being carried into the pyramid, followed by a procession

of cats and humans bearing caskets and urns brimming with treasure. There was a picture of the god Anubis welcoming Cattypuss to the underworld. There was another of the sun god Ra promising him eternal life. It was this picture that Atticus chose. He placed his paw against the hieroglyph.

The door to the tomb slid back.

Torches on the walls flickered into life.

Nobody spoke. Even the magpies were silent.

The sarcophagus stood upright on a marble podium in the centre of the tomb. Next to it was a magnificent throne. The throne was surrounded by small statues of Cattypuss the Great identical to the ones in Howard Toffly's crypt. They made a perfect circle, except that one – the one Howard Toffly had stolen – was missing.

Atticus drifted down the steps into the chamber. He felt dreamy. Treasure was piled high against the walls. It glittered and sparkled in the torchlight.

'Chaka-chaka-chaka-chaka-chaka!' From the antechamber he heard the magpies' soft chatter. They had spotted the treasure.

He approached the sarcophagus.

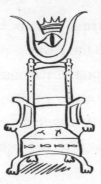 

The humans crowded round the door of the tomb, speaking in whispers.

'Is it safe to go in yet?' Lord Toffly blustered. He clutched his spoons.

Professor Verry-Clever had his eyes glued on Atticus. 'I don't know,' he admitted. 'It depends if Atticus has defeated the curse.'

'It's our treasure,' Lady Toffly sounded peeved. 'I don't see why we can't just go and get it.'

'Vy don't ve chuck the magpies in and see vot happens,' Zenia suggested. 'They shouldn't be tied up anyvay.' She glared at Biscuit. 'Release them.'

Reluctantly, Biscuit unpicked the magpies' chains one by one.

'Go on, Thug.' Jimmy gave him a shove. 'You're the expert. Go and say hi to your bessie, Anubis.'

'Goodbye, cruel world.' Thug tumbled down

the steps into the tomb. He lay there, breathing heavily, waiting for the curse to strike.

Atticus had reached the podium. He jumped on to it.

'What's he doing?' Callie whispered.

Mrs Tucker swallowed. 'I'm not sure.' She glanced at Mimi. Mimi's eyes were fixed on Atticus.

Atticus raised a paw and placed it against the sarcophagus. The door opened with a creak of its rusty hinges.

Everyone gasped.

Inside the sarcophagus was the mummy of the cat pharaoh. Upon the mummy's head rested a blue and green headdress.

Suddenly there was a swirl of dust. The torches flickered. Atticus staggered backwards. He almost fell.

'Atticus!' Mimi yowled.

Atticus didn't seem to hear her. He recovered himself. He took the headdress from the mummy, placed it on his head and leapt on to the throne. The pyramid shook.

'Oh my giddy aunt!' Mrs Tucker breathed.

'What is it?' Callie demanded.

'What's happening?' Mrs Cheddar shivered.

'I've got a nasty feeling Cattypuss the Great has taken possession of Atticus!' Mrs Tucker said. 'I've been worried something like that might happen. Is that it, Mimi? Is that what Atticus thought too?'

'Meow!' Mimi jumped into Mrs Tucker's arms to show her that she was right.

Biscuit could hardly believe his ears. *Cattypuss take possession of Atticus Claw?!* It was the most ridiculous idea he'd ever heard.

Zenia thought so too. 'Vot rot,' she shrieked. 'I've had enough of this. Biscuit! Get him!'

'My pleasure!' Biscuit growled. He'd soon show Claw who was the real king of cats around here. All the jealousy and hatred Ginger Biscuit had been bottling up burst out of him in a terrifying moan.

'MMMYYYYYYYAAAAAWWWW.'

19

Ginger Biscuit advanced on the throne.

The others watched from the doorway, horrified. They dared not move, partly in case Zenia zapped them with her hairpin pistol (which was raised and ready to fire), and partly because they were afraid. Only Mimi seemed calm. She reached out a paw to Callie and Michael to reassure them.

'You're finished, Claw.' Ginger Biscuit hopped up on to the podium and popped out his claws POP. POP. POP. POP.

Atticus glowered at him. 'WHO ARE YOU?' he thundered.

'Don't give me that,' Biscuit snarled. 'You know perfectly well who I am.' He bared his teeth. 'Your worst nightmare.'

'SILENCE!' Atticus commanded.

'You really think you're something special, don't you!' Ginger Biscuit's ears flattened against his head. 'But all you are is just a pathetic *pet*.'

'No one speaks to Cattypuss the Great, mighty ruler of Nebu-Mau, like that.' Atticus narrowed his eyes. 'You shall be punished.' He raised a paw.

'Sure!' Biscuit yawned. 'Bring it on, Claw.' He got ready to spring. 'Only there's going to be a new pharaoh in town: he's called Gingerpuss the Horrible.'

There was a sound of scratching and scurrying. 'RATS!' Lady Toffly screamed. She dropped her sack and ran back down the passageway towards the exit.

Ginger Biscuit laughed. He wasn't afraid of a few rats. He'd squish them later. 'Ooh,' he said. 'I'm really scared.'

Atticus raised his other paw.

There was a sound of clicking and buzzing.

'BEETLES!' Lord Toffly roared. He dropped his dessertspoons and ran after his wife.

Ginger Biscuit looked down. A carpet of rats surged from underneath the treasure. He looked up.

196

A plague of beetles squeezed from the cracks in the ceiling. He swallowed. Biscuit was terrified of anything spooky. And this was REALLY spooky.

Atticus raised both paws at the same time.

'SPIDERS!' Zenia Klob cried.

Huge long-legged beasts crept from the shadows to join the rats and beetles.

Ginger Biscuit started to back away.

BANG! BANG! BANG! BANG!

ZIP! ZIP! ZIP! ZIP!

Zenia waded into the tomb and started shooting hairpins at the mass of creeping animals. 'Get off my treasure,' she screeched, 'if you know vot's good for you. Ginger, kill that cat!'

Ginger Biscuit was shaking. All his bravado had disappeared.

'PHHHHOOOOOOOOOOOOOOO!' Atticus opened his mouth and blew. A stream of locusts hit Ginger Biscuit in the face. Ginger Biscuit fell off the podium into the crawling carpet.

The magpies were flying in circles around the tomb. 'Thug, me old mate!' Slasher called desperately. 'Where are you?'

A wing appeared from under some beetles,

197

followed by a sob. 'Remind me never to go tomb-raiding again.' Thug's strangled voice could be heard from beneath a very hairy spider.

BASH! SQUEAK! SQUEAK! BASH!

'We've got to stop Cattypus!' Mrs Tucker panted, kicking at the rats as they swarmed out of the tomb into the antechamber. 'Before he does anything else!'

SWAT! BUZZ! BUZZ! SWAT!

'And get Atticus back!' Mrs Cheddar swiped at the locusts with her shoe.

CLUNK! CRUNCH! CRUNCH! CLUNK!

'Youze ladies leave it to me!' Mr Tucker was doing a jig on the beetles with his wooden leg. He reached into his trouser pocket and drew out a plastic bottle. 'I knows what to do. Fetch me a tooorrrch, kids.'

Michael and Callie dodged the torrent of rats and bugs that were swarming into the antechamber. Michael lifted his younger sister up. Callie grabbed one of the flaming torches from the wall and handed it to Mr Tucker.

Mr Tucker took the stopper off the plastic bottle and hurled it into the tomb. 'Hold your noses!' he roared.

198

'Don't you mean cover your ears?' Mrs Tucker shouted back.

'No!' Mr Tucker chucked the torch in after it. 'Definitely hold your noses.'

BOOM!

A hideous smell of camel fart filled the air.

The rats, beetles and spiders scuttled for cover. They disappeared through the antechamber into the passageway, trying to find some fresh air.

'Vot is that revolting pong?' Zenia Klob struggled out of the tomb. 'Eurgh! I can't take it.' She ran after them.

'I'm out of here!' Jimmy squawked, emerging from the cloud of evil-smelling gas.

'Wait for us!' Pig, Wally and Gizzard flapped feebly after him.

'I think I'm going to be sick.' Slasher flew out.

'I want to go home!' Thug zigzagged after him. He still had a spider wrapped round his head. 'Help! I can't see!'

'MMMMYYYYAAAAWWW!' Biscuit chased off, his tail between his legs.

'Good riddance to the lot of you!' Mrs Tucker shouted after them. 'Badawi and his men will intercept them on their way out,' she added.

Just then Inspector Cheddar appeared in the antechamber. He picked a couple of rats out of his turban and removed a locust from his ear. He stumbled on in a trance, his eyes glazed. He didn't seem to smell the camel fart.

'Dad!' Michael and Callie cried.

Mrs Tucker held them back. 'He's sleepwalking,' she said. 'Don't wake him.'

'Klob's sleeping potion!' Mrs Cheddar put her hand to her mouth.

'I've come to worship the Great Cattypuss,' Inspector Cheddar announced. 'Wise and mighty ruler of Nebu-Mau.' He pushed his way through the clouds of camel fart into the tomb.

The others followed, pressing their sleeves to their noses. They looked anxiously at the podium, not knowing what to expect.

Atticus was sitting there holding his handkerchief across his nose. He wasn't wearing the cat pharaoh headdress any more.

'Look!' Michael said.

The headdress was back on the mummy. Suddenly an icy wind swept through the chamber.

The torches flickered. A terrible roar, like Biscuit's only deeper and more powerful, reverberated about the walls.

Atticus's fur blew flat.

The humans clung to one another, except Inspector Cheddar, who struggled forwards, arms outstretched.

The sarcophagus door slammed shut in a swirl of dust.

The chamber was still.

'I told youze that camel faaarrrt would come in useful!' Mr Tucker said.

Mimi jumped up beside Atticus.

'Atticus?' she said hesitantly. 'Is it really you?'

'Yes!' Atticus said. 'It's really me. That camel fart sent Cattypuss straight back to his coffin.' He laughed. 'I don't blame him. It's disgusting.' Atticus leant over so that Mimi could share his hanky to breathe through. He began to purr throatily.

'Atticus is back!' Michael cried. 'Listen!'

'It's him!' Callie gave a little scream.

Inspector Cheddar had finally made it to the throne. He knelt and clasped his hands. 'All hail the fabulous feline pharaoh of Nebu-Mau,' he said.

'Oh dear,' Mrs Cheddar sighed.

Atticus gave Inspector Cheddar a wave. He squeezed Mimi's paw. 'Isn't this great?' he said. 'Apart from the camel fart.'

'Yes,' Mimi said. 'It's absolutely brilliant to have you back.'

Atticus purred like a tractor. He'd defeated the curse, got rid of Klob, Biscuit and the Tofflys. Better still, Inspector Cheddar was worshipping him! What more could a tabby cat ask for except a plate of sardines? He looked at Mrs Tucker hopefully.

'Sorry, Atticus,' she said. 'I'm all out.'

Atticus didn't care. He'd get some when he went home. Inspector Cheddar could bring him some prawns too.

Professor Verry-Clever was inspecting the treasure. 'I propose that we take something with us to show the Egyptian authorities,' he said seriously. 'They must know what a remarkable find we've made.' He chose a gorgeous amulet and put it in his pocket with Howard Toffly's book. He stepped out of the tomb.

Suddenly the pyramid began to shake. Pieces of

stone crumbled from the walls.

'What's happening?' Mimi cried.

Atticus glanced round. It wasn't over yet. 'It's Cattypuss. He's angry. He thinks we're stealing his treasure. We must go. Now!'

20

They raced back through the passageways to the pyramid entrance. All around them stones crashed and tumbled.

Badawi and his men were waiting. They had the Tofflys but there was no sign of Klob, Biscuit and the magpies.

'Where is she?' Mrs Tucker demanded.

'I don't know,' Badawi admitted. 'The only person we saw was a man with a cart full of melons. He seemed in a real hurry.'

'That was her!' Mrs Tucker fumed. 'Biscuit and the magpies must have been hidden in the cart.'

Badawi looked crestfallen.

'Never mind,' Mrs Tucker said. 'We've got to get out of here. Cattypuss is going nuts. He's going to destroy the city.'

As she said it the statues of the
cat pharaoh started to topple one by one along the
boulevard.

'We's got to get to the baaarrrge!' Mr Tucker
limped off.

Everyone charged after him.

'I'd rather live in a caravan than stay here a
minute longer!' Lord Toffly puffed.

'I'll never complain about polishing spoons
again!' Lady Toffly sobbed.

Soon they reached the harbour. They waited
impatiently for Inspector Cheddar: he took a bit
longer than everyone else as he insisted on crawling
along on his knees after Atticus and kissing the
ground.

The other barge had already left.

'She's escaped!' Mrs Tucker cried.

'Forget Klob and grab your oooaaar, Edna,' Mr
Tucker ordered. 'This lake's choppier than a bath
full of barracuda!'

It was true. Whereas when they had arrived the
lake had been completely calm, now the wind was
whipping it into white-crested waves.

They jumped in. Atticus and Mimi helped Mr Tucker with the tiller. Everyone else took an oar. Callie and Michael had to double up because the wind was so strong. Even Badawi's warriors were having trouble.

'Heave!' Mr Tucker shouted.

They heaved.

'Heave again!' Mr Tucker roared.

They heaved again.

'Keep heaving!'

They kept heaving.

'It's no good, Herman,' Mrs Tucker shouted. They didn't seem to be getting anywhere.

'I's got more camel faaarrrt!' Mr Tucker tied it to the back of the boat. He found a match and lit it.

The barge shot forward for a few seconds. Then it stopped.

'Daaarrrn it!' Mr Tucker yelled. 'The spark's gone out.' He fumbled with his matches but they refused to light in the howling wind.

'Now what do we do?' Mrs Cheddar said.

'We must worship the righteous ruler of cats!' Inspector Cheddar bowed and scraped before Atticus.

'Only Cattypuss the Great can save us.'

Atticus was getting a bit annoyed with Inspector Cheddar now. He wished he would stop. He'd had enough worshipping for one day.

'Cattypuss must have all that he wishes!' Inspector Cheddar continued. 'For then he will look kindly upon us and help us navigate this troubled water.'

Wait a minute! Atticus jumped off the tiller. *Inspector Cheddar was right!* If they gave Cattypuss what he wanted, he'd leave them alone. The barge tipped and rolled.

'Be careful, Atticus!' Mrs Tucker shouted.

Atticus staggered over to Professor Verry-Clever and removed the amulet from his pocket with his paw. Then he picked out Howard Toffly's book with his teeth. He struggled towards the side of the barge.

'Look at Atticus!' Michael shouted.

'He's going to destroy the book!' Mrs Cheddar yelled.

'And give back the amulet!' Callie cried.

'No!' Professor Verry-Clever protested when he saw what Atticus meant to do.

I'm sorry Professor, Atticus thought. *But this is the only way.*

He threw the book as far into the lake as he could. Then he threw the amulet. The two objects disappeared in a whirl of water. But the lake didn't become calm. The waves were higher than ever.

'It's not working!' Michael yelled.

What was happening? Atticus couldn't understand. Cattypuss had the amulet. He had the book. What more could he want? Then suddenly he knew. '*He wants me!*' Atticus whispered. He stood frozen at the side of the barge. The whirlpool was approaching, whipping the waves into spray. A figure of a cat rose up out of the whirlpool, taking shape in the midst of the seething water. It towered above them, snarling. *Cattypuss!* Atticus tried to move his paws but he couldn't. Cattypuss had taken control of him again!

'Atticus!' Mimi cried. She jumped off the tiller and tried to reach him. But the barge lurched and she fell back on to Callie and Michael.

'It's that flipping cat pharaoh!' Mrs Tucker yelled. 'Somebody do something! He's going to steal Atticus!'

'We can't!' Badawi shouted. The Bedouin warriors fought with their oars, trying to stop the barge overturning.

Inspector Cheddar crawled towards the edge of the barge. He didn't notice the whirlpool. Or the snarling tower of water. He still thought Atticus was Cattypuss the Great. What he could see, though, was that the object of his worship was in danger of being knocked off the barge by a large wave. 'Oh tubby tabby of the dusty desert,' he raised his voice against the wind. 'Forgive me for putting my unworthy human hands on to your great furriness!' He gathered Atticus up and held him close to his chest.

Atticus purred throatily. On second thoughts maybe it was a good thing Inspector Cheddar was still worshipping him after all!

With a hiss of rage, Cattypuss disappeared back into the lake.

'I'm going to try lightin' me camel faaarrrt again!' Mr Tucker warned them. He put another match to the bottle.

WHIZZ! BANG!

This time the barge shot forward. Soon they

reached the golden staircase. The barge glided to a halt, slotting into the base of the stairs.

'Run!' Mrs Cheddar yelled.

They ran up the staircase and back through the tunnel of water.

'Don't look back!' Mrs Tucker ordered.

The water roared and crashed behind them.

They reached the safety of the cat's-head rocks. Slowly they turned.

'It's gone!' Callie whispered.

There was no sign of the lake. All they could see was a dry valley covered in sand.

They were all silent for a moment.

'Do you think Klob made it?' Michael asked.

Mrs Tucker snorted. 'Definitely,' she said. 'The old boot's stolen Badawi's camels.'

It was true. The camels had gone.

Badawi got out his mobile phone. 'I think we could all do with fresh ones anyway,' he said. 'And a good meal. You will be our guests for dinner tonight.'

'That sounds brilliant.' Mrs Tucker looked at Atticus. 'Do you have any sardines, Badawi?' she enquired. 'Only I think someone deserves a treat.'

21.

A few days later the travellers returned to Littleton-on-Sea. The first thing Atticus did, after eating a whole sachet of cat food and two sardines, was to put on his Police Cat Sergeant badge and visit the kittens.

Nellie Smellie was in the kitchen. She was knitting a huge jumper with her abandoned lady cats' knitting group. 'Hello, Atticus,' she said. She peered at him. 'Didn't get much of a suntan, did you?'

Atticus purred politely.

'What do you think of Mr Tucker's new jumper?' she asked. They were putting the finishing touches to the front; threading a few tasty morsels of fish into the wool.

211

Atticus purred throatily.

'I'm glad you like it,' Nellie Smellie said, giving him a bit of kipper. 'I just hope Mr Tucker manages to get it mixed up with his beard like the last one. He's not the same without his beard-jumper.'

Atticus meowed. Actually Mr Tucker had perked up a lot since their adventure. His beard had grown while they were in Egypt and he was convinced that the last bottle of camel fart he'd brought back was the missing ingredient that would make his new beard-jumper the biggest one in the world. He would be pleased to have Nellie Smellie's huge jumper to experiment with.

He padded through to the sitting room.

'Atticus!' The kittens were thrilled to see him. They sat nicely in a circle and listened without a word while he told them about his amazing journey. One of them even asked for his autograph!

'So what happened to Klob, Biscuit and the magpies?' the mean-looking kitten didn't look so mean any more. He had washed his fur and combed his tail.

'They escaped.' Atticus shrugged. 'Interpol are

still looking for them,' he said. 'They're checking their list of wanted melon sellers. I expect they'll show up somewhere sooner or later.'

'What about the Tofflys?'

'They're back at the caravan park polishing spoons. They didn't actually steal anything in the end so the Commissioner let them off with a warning.'

'What about Inspector Cheddar?'

Atticus sighed. 'He's still worshipping me,' he said. 'The doctor says it will take another week for the effects of the sleeping potion to wear off completely.'

'What did it feel like being Cattypuss the Great?' one of the kittens asked.

Atticus thought for a moment. 'There were good bits and bad bits,' he said eventually. 'A good bit was the look on Ginger Biscuit's face when I blew locusts at him. A bad bit was feeling that I didn't have any proper friends.'

Everyone was quiet for a while.

'Would you like to play a game of Monopoly?' another kitten suggested.

'I'd love to!' Atticus said.

The kittens set up the game. Nellie Smellie brought in a box of cat treats to share while they were playing.

Atticus meowed his thanks. It was good to be back home. *Friends.* He had lots of them now, Atticus realised, since he'd stopped being a cat burglar. He had the kittens and Nellie Smellie. He had Badawi and Professor Verry-Clever. He had Mr and Mrs Tucker and the children and Mimi. He had Mrs Cheddar and (for the moment at least) Inspector Cheddar. Atticus began to purr.

Forget being Cattypuss the Great, he thought happily. *I'd much rather be Atticus Grammaticus Cattypuss Claw.*